HIGH PLAINS DEATH

Johnny Faldeau had started chasing dollars by rustling and bank-busting so it had come as no great shock to find the law on his tail. But he wasn't about to give up when he had the whole of the High Plains in Texas to get lost in. What did stick in his craw, though, was the murder charge hanging over him and a waiting noose. It didn't help either that the man hot on his trail was a Yankee. The lead was surely going to fly!

ETHAN WALL

HIGH PLAINS DEATH

Complete and Unabridged

LINFORD
Leicester

First published in Great Britain in 1997 by
Robert Hale Limited
London

First Linford Edition
published 1998
by arrangement with
Robert Hale Limited
London

British Library CIP Data

Wall, Ethan
  High plains death.—Large print ed.—
Linford western library
  1. Western stories
  2. Large type books
  I. Title
  823.9'14 [F]

  ISBN 0 7089–5332–8

Published by
F. A. Thorpe (Publishing) Ltd.
Anstey, Leicestershire

Set by Words & Graphics Ltd.
Anstey, Leicestershire
Printed and bound in Great Britain by
T. J. International Ltd., Padstow, Cornwall

This book is printed on acid-free paper

For Simon and Anthony

1

Johnny Faldeau dropped to one knee and scooped up a handful of earth. As he watched the red soil of East Texas trickle through his fingers he knew he was back home. He eased himself erect, wincing and rubbing his stiff leg. He dusted his hands, took off his grey campaign hat and surveyed the cane-fields where he had played as a kid. He felt the warmth that came with recognition of familiar surroundings. The terrain of the family farm hadn't altered much since those days. Ahead was the stand of trees that had provided shade in hot summers. Beyond, just out of sight, would be the clutch of shacks his old man had built with his own hands.

It had been less than three years since he had last seen it but it seemed like a lifetime. He had left as a young man and was returning a veteran. Battle-scarred too, with a leg whose only use now was for dragging around. He hadn't mentioned that in letters to his pa. It had been a disabling injury but his pa was a fretter and he knew he would have thought it worse than it was. Anyway, there are some things you prefer to tell a loved one face to face.

He limped back to his horse, put the good leg into the stirrup and swung the stiff one over the saddle. Finally mounted, he allowed his horse to set its own pace along the final stretch.

There was a Negro labouring amongst the cane. Johnny returned the wave but didn't recognize the man. Didn't surprise him. In three years there must have been some changes in the place.

Three years, three long years. As he rode slowly through the increasingly familiar surroundings memories came flooding back. Then his mind went back to those last days just before he had donned the grey. They had been uncertain times.

Not yet a member of the Confederacy at the outbreak of hostilities Texas had not been affected by the conflict as much as the other Southern states. Even when Texas finally joined the Confederate cause, the Mississippi provided a geographical dividing line, a natural feature of the terrain which restricted the hostilities to the Eastern states. So, at least in the early stages, the war for the Lone Star State had been a distant thing. Something you talked about with neighbours but it didn't impinge too much on your daily doings.

Even so, the young Johnny had felt restless, itching to do more than talk. He'd wanted to enlist but his father persuaded him to stay on at the farm, arguing that his contribution was equally valid, helping produce the cotton that General Kirby Smith needed as barter to purchase arms and supplies through European merchants in Mexico.

Time passed in that way, in an

eerie calm, with the knowledge that things were happening elsewhere. All the same a man had to work hard. Distant though the fighting was, taxes were continually being raised to finance the war effort. Stock and produce were increasingly being commandeered to supply the CSA. And slaves were becoming more difficult to handle, sensing freedom should the Union win. When they ran, farmers and plantation owners didn't have the manpower to chase them like the old days.

The situation worsened when rumours came through that the Federals were mounting a special force in New Orleans. Under General Banks the unit had the sole objective of planting the Union flag in the Lone Star State; for the first time there was the real possibility that Texas could come under direct threat. And it didn't stay a possibility for long. Soon it was hard fact that the northerners were heading up the Red River and it was then that Johnny had defied his father and put aside his farming tools to join the Second Texas Mounted.

He'd seen his first action in Sabine country near the Louisiana border. Despite being outnumbered the Southerners had managed to repel the invaders who were on unfamiliar territory. But Confederate celebrations were short-lived. On the Cumberland and Tennessee, forts fell to the Union. Then came news of Shiloh and Vicksburg.

It was at the defence of Richmond that Johnny had been wounded. Close to an exploding artillery shell, he had sustained many injuries but the worst was his leg. It looked so bad as they stretchered him away, he thought they would have to amputate. But when he came to, the army doctor had told him they had managed to keep the limb together. From then on it would be a matter of time to see whether it would improve. That had been the good news. The bad news was Lee had pronounced defence untenable and was withdrawing his troops from the capital. Along with the other seriously wounded Johnny was to be left to the mercies of the Union.

After all the propaganda about Northerners eating babies, he was surprised to find them civilized and he was tended by their medical officers as though he was one of their own. But that didn't alter his attitude to them. They were still the enemy.

Snippets of news came into the sick bay about Lee heading south hoping to outdistance the Union forces and join other rebels for a last stand; about President Davis setting up government headquarters at Danville with the intention of continuing the war as a guerrilla operation.

But when news came through of surrender at Appomattox, the whole matter had become academic for Johnny, still laid out on his sick cot.

And he'd had to stay that way for over six months, being moved from the prison camp to a Union Army hospital. He got to know Northerners, sympathized with those who had arms and legs missing. In spirit they were not much different from himself: wounded, wanting to get back home. But their way of talking, their clipped Eastern accents, irritated him. And the gall of them, that they should try to tell the sons of Dixie how to live. But that was all behind him now like a bad dream. Or so he thought.

As he neared the stand of trees shielding the farmhouse, he saw another couple of black workers. Two more he didn't recognize. Things sure had changed around here. Had all his pa's boys been replaced?

Up close to the trees his reverie was interrupted by a voice. 'Hold it there, mister.'

He looked in the direction of the voice without checking his horse.

'I said hold it there, mister. You deaf or something?'

This time he reined in. He could make out, beside a tree, a figure training a shotgun on him. 'Lower that barrel, mister,' the weary former soldier said. 'I've had enough guns aimed in my direction to last me a lifetime.'

'State your business,' the man with the threatening weapon continued.

'Hell, I'm Johnny Faldeau.'

'Means nothing to me, mister.'

Johnny leaned forward on his saddle horn and nodded upwards. 'When I was a kid I used to have a swing from that bough just above your head. This is my pa's farm for Chrissake.'

'Not no more it ain't.'

'Since when?'

The man lowered his gun. 'Figure you're on the square.'

'Where's my pa?'

The other turned on his heel and made for the farmhouse. 'You'd better come with me.'

★ ★ ★

There were two things Johnny didn't like about the guy: pointing the business end of a shotgun at him; and the voice: it was Yankee-accented.

'There's been a lotta changes round here,' the man said when he reached the farmhouse porch.

'You're telling me,' Johnny said, swinging down from the saddle. 'Now, where's my old man?'

'If he's the guy who owned this place a way's back, he's dead.'

Eyes glazing over, Johnny looped the reins over the hitchrail like an automaton. 'Dead? How?'

'Just took sick the way I hear.'

Johnny dropped his behind onto the stoop while he absorbed the news. 'What of?'

'Don't rightly know,' the other answered.

There was silence for a spell then Johnny looked around. 'He buried on the place?'

'No. Figure they put him in the town cemetery. It all happened before I turned up.'

'Where did he die? Here?'

'No. This had ceased to be his place by then.'

'What you mean? This has been his place for twenty years. Ma's buried out back even.'

'Oh yeah, I've seen the marker. Ain't touched it. I've left it as it is.'

Johnny shook his head. 'Pa wouldn't have abandoned this place.'

'The way I heard it, he had to.'

'How come?'

'Ran into bad times. I didn't know him personally, you understand, but I got the gist from guys I trade with in town. The usual story. CSA taking most of his produce and stock. The last of his blacks scooted. The receipts the army gave him weren't worth the paper they were printed on when the Confederacy collapsed. He mortgaged the property after he saw everything vanish into the war effort, then he couldn't pay his debt charges and the bank foreclosed.'

Johnny shook his head again. 'No. I know the bank in town. Pa's dealt with them for years. They wouldn't foreclose. They would have given us breathing space. Would have waited for me to get back home at least.'

'If you're talking about that local bank in town, that collapsed too. Bunch of worthless paper and no money.'

'So who took up his debt?'

'What was left of the bank was bought over by a New York outfit.'

Johnny snorted. 'Damn carpetbaggers.'

'Call them what you like, son, but if the South is ever to get back on its feet it's Northern capital that'll do it.'

'And you bought the place from them?'

'That's the size of it.'

'At bottom dollar price too, I'll be bound.'

It was the other man's turn to shake his head. 'Southern money ain't gonna get folks out of the mess. Stuff's worthless.'

Johnny looked at him. 'And you ain't no son of Dixie either.'

'North Carolina. Born and bred. And proud of it.'

'Another damn carpetbagger.'

The other stiffened. 'I think it's time you went, mister. There's limits to my hospitality. I've done the decent thing and told you what I know.'

Johnny was thirsty and hungry. If he asked, he figured the guy would oblige but he couldn't face taking refreshment in the old kitchen with all its memories.

'Anyways,' he said, 'why did you stick a gun in my face back there? Me and Pa never had to do that to visitors. Ain't Southern hospitality.'

'You must have been out of circulation a spell. There's a wave of lawlessness spreading all over. Rangers are working at full stretch. State Legislature have even had to set up a new force, the State Police, to try to cope. Can't trust anybody riding in. Fact of the matter is the South's been wiped out. What's happened to your old man is typical. There's no money, so folk have took to stealing, robbing, rustling. An honest man's gotta defend himself and his property.'

'Like you say, things have changed.'

'If it's any consolation, you're not the only one to lose kin. My boy didn't survive Shiloh. That's one of the reasons why me and the missus moved out here. Start a new life, try to forget. Things can never be the same. Some men die in battle by a bullet, like my boy, others lose everything behind the lines, like your old man.'

The erstwhile soldier breathed deep and pulled at the beard that had decorated his features since his wounding. Despite the philosophizing the man in front of him was still a Yankee. 'Mind if I walk round and pay my respects to Ma before I go?'

The fellow nodded. 'Take your time.'

He watched Johnny get to his feet. 'Hey, son, you want a bite to eat or something?'

Johnny shook his head. 'But my hoss could do with his nose in a trough of water.'

'Leave him with me. I'll see to your mount while you pay your respects.'

2

It was late afternoon when Johnny reached Logan. He knew the town. From the farm it had been the nearest place of any size when he was growing up so he was familiar with the stores which he had visited with his folks to collect supplies. It was in one of Logan's saloons that he'd had his first drink of liquor. Boy, had that been a day to remember. But those had been special occasions, the place being just that bit too far for any regular socializing. But in those few months before he had left and was of drinking age he'd taken drinks with the town boys; that is, when the old man had allowed him respite from chores.

Whatever its former appearance, the place didn't look prosperous now. Like many Southern towns he'd ridden through. This part of Texas hadn't seen any conflict but the war had left its mark: sucking up money, resources and young men.

And it showed. Oldsters sat on boardwalks alongside young out-of-workers. He could understand down-and-out blacks. He wasn't one for politics but it had occurred to him that once slaves had been freed who would be able to afford to pay wages to blacks who had previously worked for nothing? But on the streets there were as many whites as blacks who looked homeless. Where was this new beginning Lincoln had promised?

Some asked for money as he passed. Faced with his first outstretched hand he handed over a quarter. Come the second one, he slapped his pockets and explained he was in the same boat; but the disbelief and hostility in the eyes of the pleader indicated it wasn't an acceptable response. He steeled himself to ignore subsequent entreaties.

Was this what things had come to? With his crook leg was he going to have trouble finding work too? Would he end up on some boardwalk with his hand out?

He checked his meagre resources, then took a meal at an eats house. On finishing he resumed his stroll along the boardwalks. The place had sure changed. Here and there, new names, themselves now fading, had been painted over old ones. Buildings had gone, others put up. He paused at saloon doors, looking over batwings in search of a familiar face but saw none. Three years had been a long time. Unlike well-established cities, western towns were ephemeral, folks moving on, false fronts rising, falling, changing. The young fellows he had known would have been swept up in the war themselves with all the probabilities that that carried with it: death, maiming. If not, they would have married, or simply moved on frontier-style.

He looked up at a sign reading The Forty-Five then pushed through the batwings. An old-timer sat treadling a mechanical piano and the place was well patronized but he didn't recognize anybody. At least some folks had money, judging by the busy faro, blackjack and poker tables.

He ignored a woman who smiled at him asking for a drink, and he aimed for the bar. Ahead of him a man dressed in a frock coat was clattering coins on the counter. Having completed his transaction, the man turned. He held full tankards in each hand and, so preoccupied was he in retaining their contents he didn't see Johnny. He caught the young Texan with the tankards, splashing some beer down him. Johnny stepped back, his face registering irritation as he attempted to flick away the dampness from his front. 'Hell, can't you look where you're going?'

'Sorry, mister. Just one of those things.'

Johnny ignored the apology, irritated even further when he detected yet another Yankee inflection in the voice. He cursed under his breath and bellied up to the bar to order himself a beer while the offender headed for a table behind him. The matter would have finished there but as he waited for the barman to fill his glass he heard laughter to his rear; then the clearly enunciated words: 'more Southern trash'.

He whirled round. There were four but he was in no frame of mind for counting the odds. He grabbed the nearest shoulder of the frock coat, heaving it round. 'Southern trash, eh?' he snarled at the face that he swung into view. 'I'll give you 'southern trash', you Yankee carpetbagger.'

Anger against the Northern takeover of his country had been brimming up in him for a long time; and what he had come home to had brought his feelings to a head. His pent-up emotions were all summed up in the fist that he stabbed plumb into the man's jaw.

Man and chair crashed to the floor

under the impact, table and drinks overturning in the débâcle.

One of the four was too liquored-up to react and sprawled to the boards in a drunken stupor; but the other two managed to pull themselves away in time to avoid the crashing table.

'Hell, ain't no cause for that,' the nearest one said. 'Let's calm down a mite, Reb.' His tone was placating but, in turning to face the Southerner in apparent meekness, his hidden right arm had begun a swing. However, Johnny expected it was coming, and was already hurling out his own fist. He missed the chin but in the sweep his elbow caught his attacker in the throat, an impact which had the man gagging. While he dropped to his knees the other moved forward but Johnny's left was already cartwheeling and, although not a solid blow on target, shoved the fellow backwards.

The action had spun Johnny so his back was to the one he had first downed. The man was still not fully recovered but had enough resources to make a grab at Johnny from the rear. Johnny elbowed backwards, this time banging the wind out of the man.

The music had stopped and a hush had fallen over the establishment as folk backed away to watch the fun from a safe distance.

Now free, the Southerner whirled round 180 degrees bringing up his boot in harmony with the turn and smashed the man in his midriff. As he straightened, another tried to give him a bear hug from the side but he bent from the waist slinging the man over. The movement spun him round and he took the impact of another who shouldered him in the chest. They locked together in an awkward dance until his attacker broke free and slung a right sending Johnny staggering backwards. He looked clumsy yet he kept to his feet and met the man's second charge.

Bent double by the impact he threw his arm around the man's waist and the two crashed to the floor. He pulled himself free from his winded assailant but, only managing to get to all fours, he was vulnerable to the flying kick of another which caught him in the belt region, spinning him over on the boards. Face down he felt the man leap onto his back. In a tangle of arms and legs he managed to worm himself over so that his own back was pressed against the boards, but the new position allowed his assailant to wrench at his jaw. He felt nails gouging into his flesh and was aware of gristle crunching at the hinge of his jawbone. The hand was groping around his distorted mouth and he bit into the first available finger.

The fellow roared with pain and Johnny took advantage of his faltering to fling his head upwards cracking the man on the nose. Momentarily neutralized the man could be kneed away with a raised leg which Johnny did only to find the bozo replaced by another who dropped on him like a ton of Longhorn bull. As they moved in a bear-hug roll across the floor the one with the bloodied nose fell against the wall alongside the drunken fourth member who had taken no part in the shindig, merely watching the proceedings with a bemused expression on his face.

The other felt his pained nose, examined the blood on his hand then looked back at Johnny who had now managed to get the top position in his present coupling. The exposed back was too much of an invitation. He blew gouts of blood from his nose and rose, pulling his gun. Anticipation of satisfaction was in his eyes but his face changed when he felt something cold and hard in the back of his neck, a sensation that was accompanied by an ominous click.

Head and widening eyes turned to see the most wrinkled face he had ever seen. Ancient eyes flicked, an old head shook and the mouth embedded in the grizzled whiskers mouthed a silent 'No'. While he was taking the message in, the pistol that was trained on him rose quicker than his eyes could register and chopped the side of his skull; and he returned, this time unconscious, to the floor beside his drunken partner.

Meanwhile Johnny had got his hands around the throat of his current opponent. He was getting a lot of satisfaction from rhythmically banging the man's head against the boards and was unaware that the remaining one was rising behind him. The unseen man hurled himself forwards knocking the Texan off balance. Then the two of them held him pinioned, one on each arm.

But only for a few seconds. As one swung a heavy punch downwards Johnny twisted his head so that the fist, rammed knuckle down at full force, met hard wood. With a contorted face, the man relaxed his grip of the arm. That was enough for Johnny to use the freed arm to be used in an upward punch that thudded into the face of the other.

Johnny heaved himself upwards and cracked a second fist into the man, the impact of which sent the fellow backwards, only to receive Johnny's weight coming at him at a run. Despite the momentum the two managed to stay on their feet, but the action took both of them the short distance across the room and crashing through the batwings. Across the boardwalk they went and toppled into the street.

With onlookers jamming themselves in the door in their attempt to continue watching the free entertainment, Johnny heaved the man to his feet by his shirt and put three punches into the hated Northern face. Dealt hard and consecutively the blows were enough to put the man out. Johnny let go the shirt allowing the man to crumple to the ground. For a moment he stood, bent forward, hands on knees, panting, staring at the still form beneath him.

Then he rose and turned. Onlookers scattered as the fourth drunken Northerner bungled his way through the batwings. He teetered on the edge of the boardwalk, eyes flickering, trying to make sense of the scene.

'You want some tangling with Southern trash?' Johnny snarled breathlessly.

The man blinked like his brain was somewhere else. 'No, sir,' he slurred. 'I didn't call you no names, mister.'

Johnny stepped up onto the boardwalk alongside him. 'Well, git,' he said, giving the drunk a half-hearted push with one hand which was enough to trigger him into toppling down the steps and pitching into the dirt of the street.

Johnny pushed his weary body through the batwings. Still breathing hard he lumbered across the floor looking for number three and found him still slumped against the wall.

He noted the rising lump on the side of the forehead of the man he sought and the gun, an antiquated Dragoon, firmly in the grip of the old man seated beside him.

The oldster saw the question in Johnny's eyes, nodded to another pistol safely out of harm's way on the table, and said, 'Ain't fair a man pulling a gun in a fist fight. No Southern gentleman would have tried to break the rules like that.'

There was a hint of Irish brogue in the voice.

'You're not Southern,' Johnny said.

'That I am, my boyo. Southern Irish!'

Johnny nodded a thank you and looked around, doing a mental count of the opposition. Coming to four and satisfying himself they were all accounted for, he scanned around for his hat. He picked it up, dusted it against his trousers and took it to the bar where he slumped on his elbows, breathing hard.

The music jerked back into life and the buzz of conversation returned.

He worked his jaw sideways, and felt

it where it had been wrenched. Then he looked at his face in the bar mirror and attempted to wipe away blood and sweat. That little fandango had got something out of his system. He ran his hand down his crook leg. He felt some discomfort but, by jiminy, it hadn't let him down. Hey, things were getting better.

He walked along the bar, retrieved his beer and took a swig.

'Welcome home, son,' he heard at his side.

He glanced in the voice's direction. It was the old man again.

'I know you?'

'Not intimately. I knowed your old man better.'

Johnny studied him, some kind of memory glimmering in his brain. 'Yeah, you're . . . ' But no name came.

'Anxiety Jones.'

'Yeah. That's it. Anxiety Jones. Always thought as a kid what a funny name for a guy.' He mused on it. 'Yeah. You helped Pa with chores on the farm.'

'That I did. The man was good enough to employ me from time to time.'

Further recollections came to the young man. 'You stayed over once and looked after him when he had a dose of fever. I remember that too.'

The oldster shrugged. 'A feller does what he can.'

'How you doing?' Johnny asked, his demeanour brightening.

'Not badly at all, kid. Heard the scuttlebutt you'd got back. Folks saw you ride through this morning.'

'So someone remembers me. Was beginning to think I was in a foreign country.'

'No, you ain't been forgotten. But there's been a lotta changes. Say, sorry about your pa.'

Johnny nodded.

'Anyways,' the oldster continued, 'what was that all about?'

'Yankees shooting their mouths off.'

Anxiety took out a stub of cigarette from his pocket, lit it and coughed. 'Thought we'd got the war on our hands all over again. Ha, when locals saw it was a Reb against Yanks they was a-gonna join in but they got stopped.'

'Who by?'

'The boss.' The oldster threw a glance at a man seated at the far end of the room. The fellow was well dressed, sporting an ornate vest with a golden chain.

'Glad he did,' Johnny said. 'Didn't want nobody butting in. That was my personal shindig.' He finished off his drink. 'Anyways, if he put money on the other guys, tell him I'm sorry he lost his bet.'

'No, he didn't stop the crowding in because of a bet. He wanted to see how you fared.'

'He did, eh? What's his interest?'

'He likes to see how a guy can handle himself. Anyways, getting down to practicalities, where are you staying? I know you've lost your place.'

'Ain't fixed up yet. Have to be a drover's cot. I'm strapped.'

'There's a room at my place if you've a mind. A little adobe just outa town. Ain't much but it's home as they say.'

The young man grinned a humourless grin. 'I ain't got the dollars to pay my way.'

'Johnny, you'll be my guest. Some-wheres to lay your head until you've sorted out what you're gonna do.'

'I'm obliged, Mr Jones.'

'Right, that's settled. And you call me Anxiety.' He looked at the back of the saloon and saw the fine-suited fellow beckon. 'Now come over, looks like the boss wants to meet you.'

Johnny shrugged. 'I can do with getting my butt on a chair.'

Anxiety caught the barman's eye, gestured for drinks and led Johnny to the table.

'Quite a show you put on there,' the finely dressed gent said. He put out a hand. 'Hal Wallace's the name.'

The other took the hand. 'Johnny Faldeau.'

'Yes, I know. Come, sit down.'

The two made themselves comfortable.

'You the boss around here then?' Johnny said.

'Boss, owner, what you will. Anxiety here told me about you coming back to troubles.'

'Troubles, yeah, you can say that again.'

'Sorry about your father.'

'Thanks.'

'Didn't know him myself but Anxiety tells me he was a good man.'

'That he was.'

The fresh drinks arrived and Johnny took a mouthful. 'Things have real changed around here. Damn Yankees all over the place.'

'It's called Reconstruction.'

'Whatever it's called, I don't like it.'

'We are of one mind there, Johnny.' He stood up. 'Now, if you'll excuse us, Anxiety and I have got some business to attend to. Can I trust you not to go butting any more Yankee heads? I'd like to keep some furniture intact.'

'As long as they keep their traps shut.'

'OK, have a good time, Johnny. The drinks are on the house.'

Johnny raised his glass. 'Gee, thanks, Mr Wallace.'

'Please, call me Hal.'

Anxiety rose to join his boss who was now walking away. 'See you later, Johnny, and we'll mosey back to my place.'

3

The place was a roughly executed adobe clinging to a slope with a couple of adjoining lean-tos. Behind it, a rise with trees screened it from north winds.

Johnny and the old-timer came up the dirt track from town. They unhorsed and hitched their animals to a small rickety fence.

'We'll stable them later,' Anxiety said, pointing to one of the lean-tos. 'There should be enough room in the big one for two horses.'

As the two men mounted the weed-fringed stoop a young girl came to the door. She was slender with auburn hair pulled together in a neat, wisping chignon. 'Gonna have to make the vittles spread to three tonight, lass,' the oldster said.

The girl looked at the visitor with

guarded curiosity.

'Name's Faldeau,' Anxiety explained.
'Johnny Faldeau. Knew his pa. And
him too when he was a young
whipper-snapper.'

As he spoke he noticed Johnny's
expression reciprocating the curiosity.

'This, Johnny, is Veener, my daughter.'

Johnny took off his hat, surprise still
writ large on his features. 'Pleased to
meet you, miss.'

'Ain't she a looker?' Anxiety smiled.

She smiled with a touch of embarrassment and led the way inside.

'You didn't say nothing about no
daughter,' Johnny said under his breath,
equally embarrassed, as he followed his
host inside.

★ ★ ★

'What kind of war you have, Johnny?'

It was evening and they were each
tackling a generous plateload of schnitzel
with assorted vegetables.

'I was doing OK till Richmond.

Then the Yankees began pressing down devilish hard. Lee was debating how long we could hold out. We were hoping for reinforcements but as the days passed it was becoming clear there wouldn't be any. Then I had an argument with an artillery shell during the siege. Got smashed up pretty bad.'

Anxiety nodded. 'I see'd you wus packing a crook leg. Didn't remember you having that encumbrance when you were a younker.'

'God knows how the sawbones put it back together but they did. Then it was while I was flat on my back that the Yankees were moving in to completely surround the capital. When they finally broke through into the suburbs Lee made the decision to evacuate. Our boys had to move pretty fast if they were to remain a fighting force so it meant leaving the hospitals to the Yankees.'

'How's they treat yuh?'

'Well enough, I figure. But they were

still Yanks. Anyways, that's how I saw the war out.'

He took a bite of the crispy meat, chewed a spell then asked, 'How about you?'

'Tried volunteering but they took one look at my grey beard and sent me on my way.' He chuckled. 'I figured my military experience would outweigh my age but they wouldn't have none of it.'

'What military experience was that?'

'Mexican War,' Anxiety declared proudly. 'Missourian regiment. Fought alongside Colonel Alexander Doniphan hisself. Chased the enemy clear out of Texas right back to Chihuahua. Pity Old Alex wasn't back in the saddle when the War Between the States broke out. He'd have found a place for an old campaigner like me. Would have been better than swamping saloons for the duration in a no-horse town like Logan.'

'So, what was it like behind the lines?'

'Chaos. Prices went through the clouds. A lotta folks realized from the outset it was just a matter of time before the Yankees won. The bluebellies had more men, better equipment. They were blockading the ports so our stuff wasn't getting in or out. We couldn't export the cotton or get outside armaments.'

'I've heard all that before but we had a helluva an advantage in our men. You couldn't see that unless you were in the ranks. Our boys had heart, they wanted to fight, while the Yankee regiments were made up of conscripts with their minds on getting back home to their soft lives. And they was mainly city boys. Used to being cooped up in factories. Ours were men of the land, used to existing on the land. And most of 'em were brung up with a gun in their hand. Most of the Yanks hadn't seen a gun until they'd got a uniform on their back.'

'Yeah,' the old man acknowledged, 'that would account how-come our forces held out so long against the odds. But a lotta folks back home saw the writing on the wall early on.' He grunted. 'The blacks figured which way to lay their chips mighty quick and started skedaddling. So we had vast tracts of land and no labour to work it: white boys fighting, blacks freeing themselves and heading north. Upshot was food became scarce, cotton rotted, fertile land didn't get seeded. There was nobody to hold the herds so the cattle began scattering all over Texas and growing wild. Hell, lotta folks died; infants, the old, simply 'cause they hadn't got vittles in their bellies. Just like the boglands in the forties all over again. It was a crying shame. Lotta folks went the same way as your pa.'

Johnny breathed deeply, reflected, then, 'Well, it's over.'

'Trouble is, now it's over — it's not really over. Carpetbaggers all over the place. Yankees in all the seats of power running the Lone Star.'

'Yeah. And freed blacks everywhere I look. Can't get over that. Suppose they'll be giving 'em the vote next. The world's going crazy.'

'Don't bad-mouth the black man, son. Society is made up of a patchwork quilt of different kind of folk. Some guys get into the habit of picking on smaller groups as the cause of their own ailments. I know: as a Paddy I've been on the receiving end. I've seen it happen to Jews too. In these parts the rednecks, they hate Mexes. There's good and bad in all races, son.'

Johnny reluctantly gave a nod and changed the subject. 'How did you get by during the conflict?'

'Well, I'd just got the mud hut. No stock. Nothing that the CSA saw worth commandeering. So they left me alone and at least I had a roof over my head. Things got pretty bad until I started working for Wallace.'

'Doing what?'

'Well, when war breaks out little cracks start appearing in what you

40

might call the fabric of everyday affairs. Wallace had a genius for filling 'em. Still has.'

Johnny spiked a potato and munched on it. 'Yeah, I can see it must have been pretty bad with no land, no money, and a young girl to look after.'

There was silence and looks were exchanged between father and daughter.

'My father is a little embarrassed to recount that aspect of our family history,' the girl interjected, 'but I don't think he'd mind if I explained.'

The old man nodded and the girl continued, 'You see, I haven't been here in Logan very long. Ma and I lived in New England. During the war we were living the soft city life you described.'

'I didn't mean soft life in any derogatory sense, miss,' Johnny said in a fluster. His embarrassment at being in the presence of a comely looking young maiden now compounded by her seeming reproach.

'Not to mind,' she said. 'Continuing

my story, Ma fell ill. Then, not long ago, she died. Consumption. I was suddenly alone and it occurred to me it was about time I sought Pa out. Patch up whatever differences we had between us.'

The old man smiled a sad smile. 'There were no differences between us, lass.'

He looked at the young man. 'Fact is, Johnny, I've always been fiddle-footed. Couldn't stand being cramped up. I left home when Veener was young. I was a bastard.' He looked at his girl. 'Excuse the language, lass, but it's true. I deserted my family and left them to fend for themselves. Came West to start a new life. Huh, made a mess of that, too. Then suddenly, a few months ago, this beautiful, full-growed woman was standing on the stoop. Didn't recognize her at first. How she found my where-at I don't know.' He squeezed her hand. 'But glad she did. She's all I got.' He looked at her, moisture in his eyes. 'Makes me realize life ain't been so bad after all.'

Veener put her other hand on his hand and returned the clench, then rose. 'Listen, you two men take a sit-down on the porch while I make coffee and clear up.'

★ ★ ★

Some ten minutes later they were seated outside listening to the symphony of night insects and looking at the lights of the not-too-distant town.

Johnny took a sip of the coffee that Veener had just brought out. 'That meal sure was delicious, Veener. What was it?'

'Schnitzel. It was a staple meal cooked by my mother.'

Johnny patted his stomach. 'Been a long time since I had such a pleasurable meal.'

'Thank you.'

He watched her go inside. He turned and realized the old man had caught his overlong glance at his daughter.

'Say, how did you pick up your come-by name?' Johnny asked in an attempt to dislodge the notion that had obviously sprung to both their minds. 'I always wondered as a kid. Fact, I'm still wondering.'

'Anxiety?' the old man said with a chuckle. 'Figure it's because nothing seemed to worry me. Whenever there's been trouble I couldn't handle I've skedaddled.'

Johnny looked at the wrinkled face in the light of the oil-lamp and reckoned if the man wasn't a fretter he sure had the appearance of one — with a brow that looked like a ploughed field — but he said nothing.

'Ain't the most responsible way of living,' the old man continued, 'but it's the way I've always been. That's how come I'm on this side of the water. Irish potato famine back in the forties. I was one of the lucky ones to get out. Made it to Liverpool. It was only a few pence for passage on a packet. But conditions were atrocious. Liverpool was full of starving Irish refugees. Thousands. Two families to a room. Many had fever. Rents went through the roof. On top of everything else the Liverpool folk became antagonistic, so I upped stakes, managed to get passage on an Atlantic boat. But New York was as bad as Liverpool. Crowded with immigrants, mainly from the Emerald Isle. There was a heap of bad feeling there too. Anyways, that's where I met Veener's ma.'

'She Irish?'

'No, Austrian. Olga, her name was. She come over because of troubles in Vienna. You know what them Continental countries are like — a revolution every fortnight. But I never understood too much about it; the English language was never her strong point.' He chuckled when he thought about it. 'Jehosophat, I tried to teach her so she knew some words, but when she used them they never seemed to come out in a way that made much sense. Anyways, as far as I could make out her family was associated with some revolutionaries but their fortunes were reversed when Francis Joseph took over.

'There was just her and her folks making it to the States. None could speak a word of English. You know, on the quays in New York they had these guys called runners. For a small fee they would volunteer to take an immigrant to a lodging-place and when they got the poor bastards there they simply stripped them of everything they had brought over and turfed them out in the street. Could you believe that, after all they'd been through?

'Cut a long story short, I took a shine to Olga and asked for her hand in marriage. I'd been in New York long enough to know the ropes and had got a place. Her folks had enough burdens and were glad to get her off their hands. You might not believe it, younker, but I was a good-looking feller in my youth.

'I called her Veener — that was

the way she pronounced Vienna and I didn't cotton to the name Olga, helluva ugly moniker for a female, don't you think? Anyways, after a spell, Little Veener came along and things went OK for a while. But there was a slump, I lost my job, couldn't handle the bills. I liked the situation less and less and, as I'd got used to doing when surrounded by problems, I lit out. Wrong, I know, but that's the way I am.' He looked back at his ramshackle dwelling. 'I'd have lit out from here ages back if there'd been any place else to go to. Good job I didn't, or Little Veener wouldn't have found me.'

'What's she intending to do now she has found her long lost pa?'

'Hasn't said. Seems to get a kick out of looking after me at the moment. But I can look after her too now in my own way. Make good dollars with Wallace. Got a little stashed by, so she can have that when the Good Lord decides it's time for me to start pushing up daisies.

Makes me feel good, I can make up to her a little for deserting her when she was young.'

He looked away, to hide the moisture returning to his eyes. 'Just a pity, it's too late I can't make it up to her ma in the same way.'

4

The next morning Johnny rose early before the others. The previous day's scrap was now exacting its toll from his body, particularly the leg. Only time could handle that but he could do something about the dirty-looking face that had looked back at him from the mottled mirror on the wall. Unable to find much water in the kitchen, he went outside and scouted for a well round the perimeter of the place, still without success.

'You're up early,' he heard from the doorway. It was Veener, watching him as she tidied her hair.

If anything she looked more beautiful in the morning light. 'What do you do for water around the place?' he asked. He'd hoped he could have grabbed a wash down before she saw him.

'Nearest pump is the blacksmith's on

the edge of town. He lets us draw as much as we like.'

He looked down at the town to remind himself of the distance and grimaced good-humouredly.

'I know,' she said. 'That's what I thought too.'

He noticed the way her pretty mouth moved slightly to the side as she smiled.

'What do you carry it in?' he asked.

She retired inside and quickly emerged with a carrying bar and a couple of pails.

By the time he had collected a couple of loads and trudged back up the rise, Anxiety was on the stoop. 'Sleep well, young un?'

'Sure did.' He hadn't slept well. Coming to terms with his father's death and the shock of being flat-as-a-flapjack broke hadn't made for relaxation, despite his tiredness. But there was no reason to whine to the man who was being kind to him. 'What you're doing is well appreciated,

Anxiety. I'll see you're not out of pocket once I'm back on my feet.'

The elder dismissed the offer with a firm gesture. 'You'll do no such thing.'

Johnny put down the pails to rest. 'Well, I can sure help out with chores. Fetch water, chop stovewood, clear brush.'

'Now that I won't argue with, younker.'

Hearing the voices, Veener had come to the door. 'You know, Pa,' she said, 'under all that hair, dirt and bruising it could be quite a handsome fellow you've brought home.'

The two men exchanged glances as she took a pail inside.

★ ★ ★

After a sorely needed wash down Johnny found himself sitting before a large breakfast. Anxiety's hospitality was helping take some of the edge off squaring up to his misfortunes. It made him feel good that the squashing of the Confederacy hadn't wiped out all the old Southern virtues, even if they were being exhibited by an Irishman. When he was back on his feet he would repay the oldster for his kindness.

'What are your plans?' Anxiety asked when they were well into their meal.

Johnny glanced out of the window. 'First off I'd like to see Pa's grave. Whereabouts is the cemetery?'

The other explained, then said, 'I have to go to town myself. If you like I'll see you later in the Forty-Five for a shot of anti-temperance fluid.'

Veener tutted as she finished her meal and neatly placed her knife and fork alongside the empty plate. 'Now don't get our young friend into the bad habit of drinking early in the day.'

Anxiety grinned as he took out the makings. 'What do you think about that? Only been here a couple of weeks and she's ordering her old man about already!'

She looked at him fiddling with

tobacco and paper. 'And those things aren't going to make your cough any better either.'

* * *

It wasn't long before Johnny had walked the short distance to the cemetery at the other end of town. He soon found the simple wooden cross that marked his father's grave. The lettering was crudely burnt: Edward Faldeau, 1865. There were no maudlin sentiments on the marker; and no age was given; there was nobody to reckon the years. He took off his hat and stood before it for a few minutes in wet-eyed remembrance. The fellow had been a cantankerous old buzzard at times, but the oldster had been his pa and there had been love between man and boy.

He pulled his emotions together and walked back to town, heading for the shingle that marked Doc Thompson's. He was the only medic in town and had tended his ma during her last days. As Johnny stood on the doorstep he shuddered inside when he recalled having been hauled there as a screaming kid for stitches in a hand he had sliced with a blade in the field.

'I called to ask about my pa,' he said when he was called into the examination room. 'Ted Faldeau. Died a spell back.'

The doctor looked over his spectacles seeking to identify the man before him. Then, 'Ha, yes. You must be . . . '

But he couldn't recall the name and the young man helped him out. 'Johnny.'

'Ha, yes. Johnny. Went off to war, didn't you? Not long after your ma had passed on as I remember. Very sad.'

'The thing is, Doctor Thompson, I've only just got back and learned about Pa. What can you tell me about his passing?'

'Old fellow got took with pneumonia. I did my best for him but he was far gone by the time I saw him. His heart wasn't in surviving. Didn't get over losing the farm. Happened to so many. The war hit many at home as well as those who went off with a rifle. With your ma gone there was only you left. When you reach a certain age and circumstances the only thing you think about is leaving something for your young. When he lost that, I think he lost the strength to fight illness.'

He enquired how the young man had fared, what kind of war he had had. Then Johnny asked if there was anything owing on his pa and the doctor waved a dismissive hand. 'Only sad I couldn't help your pa pull through.'

Johnny thanked him, shook his hand and made his way out. In the waiting-room he caught sight of himself in the mirror, reminding him he hadn't had his hair cut since way back in the army hospital.

Outside once more he made for the striped pole. The barber remembered him and his old man so there was no shortage of topics as his hair was trimmed.

'You want me to fetch that beard off?' the hair-artist said as he finished. 'Never looks good on a young man.'

Johnny raised a staying hand. 'No. I've gotten used to it. How much do I owe you?'

'For a returning veteran, Johnny, on the house.'

★ ★ ★

His grooming session over Johnny walked across to the Forty-Five where Anxiety was leaning on the rail outside. 'Come inside, Johnny. Mr Wallace would like to see you.'

'What's it all about?'

'I told you he's my boss. Well, he's looking for a new hand. When I told him I knew you — knew you was a reliable kid — he got interested.'

Inside they joined Wallace at a table. 'What you been up to, Johnny?' the saloon owner asked after he had ordered drinks.

'Took a look at the old man's grave.

56

Had a word with the doc about his passing.'

Wallace nodded. 'And what are your plans now?'

'Must confess, Mr Wallace, ain't got my brain around anything yet. Losing Pa's just sinking in.'

'I hear you've bunked down at Anxiety's place?'

'Yeah.'

'That's convenient.' Wallace waited until shot glasses and a bottle were on the table. He poured slugs all round, and indicated the full glasses to the other two. 'Enjoy yourself last night, Johnny?'

'Yeah, sure, Mr Wallace. Thanks for the hospitality.'

'Don't mention it, Johnny.'

'Here's your health, sir,' Johnny said, raising his glass.

Wallace followed suit. 'Gentlemen both — yours, and better luck still.'

The young man sipped his whiskey and returned his glass to the table. 'I'm obliged but sure don't know why you're so hospitable to a stranger.'

'You ain't a stranger, Johnny. Anxiety is kinda family round here, and he knew you and your pa. Anyway, the day a Southerner can't buy a few drinks for a fellow Southerner when he's in a hole will be a bad day for Dixie.' He flicked his eyes to the scene of Johnny's scrapping the previous day. 'Besides, I like the way you wouldn't take any bad-mouthing from the carpetbaggers. I take their money but don't mean I have to love 'em.'

'Damn Yankees deserve all the misfortune they get.'

Wallace chuckled. 'We got a lot in common, Johnny.' He kept his eyes on those of the young man as he continued, 'You killed yourself any Yankees, Johnny?'

For a second Johnny was thrown by the question. Then came back with, 'I put in three years soldiering on the front line, Mr Wallace. I got my share.'

'How many you kill?'

'You ain't been in uniform, have you, Mr Wallace?'

'No. The way it fell, my contribution to the war effort was keeping the wheels of commerce rolling. Ain't that so, Anxiety?'

Anxiety nodded.

'Well, if you don't mind me saying so, Mr Wallace, not being in the front line shows by your question,' Johnny went on. 'You see a soldier, leastways most soldiers, don't keep a tally. Anxiety here will bear me out. He's done his share. It's a job they're doing. That's it. You don't think about the enemy as people. Otherwise a feller could have trouble doing what he's gotta do. You just do it, and try to forget about it. After you've seen a few men drop under the muzzle of your gun you stop counting. When it's done, it's behind you.'

'The kid's right,' Anxiety said. 'I can't say how many Mexes I got notched on my fowling-piece.'

Wallace took a drink, studying the

young man. 'Well, Johnny, I need men with guts. The kinda guts that is shown by a guy with three years hard soldiering under his belt.'

Johnny said nothing so Wallace added, 'Men like you.'

'For what?'

'This and that.'

'That's still muddy water; don't explain much.'

'A guy's gotta be careful until he knows about a guy.'

'Which guy you talking of?'

'I'm talking about you, Johnny.'

'Go on.'

'You're broke.'

Johnny shrugged in acceptance of the statement.

'And you don't like Yankees.'

'If they all got packed back across the Mason-Dixon line it wouldn't be early enough for me.'

'And you know how to handle yourself. I saw that last night.'

'Where's all this leading, Mr Wallace?'

'Like I been trying to tell you I'd

like you in my outfit. You wanna make some money, don't you?'

'The saloon business? What do I know about that?'

'No. I have other operations going. How d'you feel about the law, Johnny?' He swivelled his hand at the wrist one way then the other. 'I mean bending it.'

'As far as I can make out under this Reconstruction malarkey the Federals have had a hand in setting up Texas's new law agencies. That makes 'em Yankee laws in my book.'

'Well, these operations of mine, they all work on the same principle. Like Robin Hood. You know, taking money from the ones who don't deserve it and putting it in the pockets of those who do.'

'And who are these two parties?'

'On the one hand, Yankee carpet-baggers, like the ones you were pulling down on last night, on the other, deserving Southerners.'

'And who are these deserving Southerners?'

'Me, Anxiety and the boys. And you, if you're in.'

'Tell me more.'

'Only if you're in.'

'Suits me. I'm in.'

Wallace drew on his cigar. 'I notice you're a mite stiff in the leg. That hold you back some?'

'Got that fighting for the flag. I can still butt a saddle.'

'And didn't seem to encumber you much last night either. What you like with cattle?'

'Ain't been a full-time puncher but I've handled stock on the farm and in the army.'

'Good.'

'Why'd you ask?'

'Well, I've got a couple of jobs lined up. One's tonight. There's five of us but I'd feel better with another pair of hands. Moving beef. Not too many but it'll be at night. You got anything against night work?'

'Over the last three years I've had to do a lotta things at night.'

'You know the Lazy Anchor?'

'No.'

'No, reckon you wouldn't if you been away for a few years. Pretty new set-up. Anyway, it's Yankee-owned but it's crewed by local boys. Some of 'em are pals of mine and they're gonna cut out a passel of cows tonight. Gonna graze 'em at an agreed point five miles out from the main herd. All we gotta do is ride out and pick 'em up. That way the working punchers are in the clear. They just report back to their foreman about the rustling. There's only half a dozen of the boys and they'll spin a tale about being jumped and outnumbered.

'Then we fog the beeves to a rendezvous on the county line where's there's another outfit who will be waiting to take 'em off our hands. Easy as pie. Won't take more than six hours riding. Nice and easy. We get back in the early hours of the morning and make ourselves seen in town so we're in the clear too. Nobody hurt. Nobody suspicious. Just dough in our hands.'

'And what about the dough?'

'All been arranged: a two-way split between the punchers and us. On this particular operation we don't come out with big potatoes. It's just something to keep us occupied in between big jobs. But you'll make yourself a neat profit for a night's work and that's what you want, ain't it — dollars in your pocket?'

Johnny nodded.

'OK,' Wallace said, raising his glass. 'Welcome to the outfit, Johnny.'

Johnny reciprocated by raising his glass and clinking it against the other's.

Wallace raised his hands to encompass his surroundings. 'This is the perfect cover. I'm a respectable businessman. Pay my taxes. And running this place I can see the boys when necessary to fix jobs without raising any suspicions. They come and go just like ordinary waddies. They have a drink, play cards, take a woman when they're inclined, and nobody is any the wiser. Had a good little number here for some time, ain't we, Anxiety?'

The oldster nodded.

They drank, then Wallace observed, 'I see you don't carry a gun, Johnny. Is that wise in these fractious days?'

'I think I can handle myself without one.'

Wallace smiled. 'Judging by yesterday's performance, I figure you can.'

'You say you got two jobs in the pipeline?' Johnny went on.

'Yeah. The next one's some days away. You'd like that one too. And that is big potatoes. But I'll tell you about that when we get closer to the time.'

He rose. 'Anyways, stick around. The rest of the boys'll be coming in later. I'll introduce you.'

5

Johnny was killing time playing draw poker with some locals in the Forty-Five. It was a small pot game; he won some, lost some.

Suddenly the bartender was at his side. 'Mr Wallace wants you in back.'

Johnny folded his cards. 'It was a bum hand anyhows.' He pushed his cents towards the middle of the table. 'Excuse me, gentlemen. Enjoyed the play and your company.'

At the back room Wallace ushered him through the door. There were three men taking their ease.

'These are the boys,' Wallace said, closing the door. 'Dave. Mort.' He indicated them in turn.

Mort had a shock of white hair, despite not being much over thirty. Dave was shorter and somewhat younger, maybe Johnny's age. His hair being cropped close to his skull gave emphasis to a jagged white scar running across the top of his head.

'You'll have something in common with them,' Wallace added. 'They rode with Quantrill's Raiders.'

Johnny nodded in acceptance of the information but made no comment. If the fact was supposed to put them in well with him, it didn't. Quantrill's outfit had not been a bona fide part of the CSA. A casual outfit that operated to its own rules, it rode sorties into Federal territory terrorizing the countryside. Some saw it as doing a useful job, putting the fear of God into Northern civilians and thus sapping the morale of Union soldiers. Least, that was the claimed idea. Others, and Johnny was one of them, saw it for what it was: a gang of renegades using the Confederate Jack as an excuse for rape and pillage. The massacre at Lawrence when 150 ordinary folk had been bloodily butchered was a stain on the flag under which they claimed to ride.

But he wasn't going to pick at the sore.

The only one of the three to give more than a nod of acknowledgement when being introduced to the newcomer was Lenny. Initially with his back to the door he turned and grinned a 'Welcome aboard' through a droop moustache and put out his hand. His words and the short pigtail at the back of his neck together with the tattoo of a clipper on his extended forearm declared he was no stranger to the sea.

Johnny shook the hand. 'Howdy.'

'As you've gathered,' Wallace went on, 'Anxiety is my number one. When I'm not around you take your orders from him. Mort is our sharpshooter. Not that we use gunplay but it's kind of his hobby and there ain't nothing he don't know about guns. Dave doesn't look it but he's the educated one amongst us. That means he can read. Knows his horses too. And Lenny, well, he's our jack-of-all-trades. But one thing they've all got in common, they're all good boys.'

'That's us neatly catalogued up,' Mort said, his face and voice stiff, 'but what about him?'

Wallace grinned. 'Necessity is the mother of invention.'

'That means he's broke,' Dave explained in response to the perplexed look that came over Mort's features.

'And he don't mind taking from Yanks,' Wallace added. 'Anyways, I've said we need another on the team and I'm sure Johnny's our boy.'

'Can we trust him?'

'We can trust him,' Anxiety said. 'Knew his pa. Johnny is a chip off the old block.'

'Got a good war record too,' Wallace added. 'Got some Yankees notched on his belt.' He crossed the room and sat down at the table. 'Well now we all know each other, let's get down to business. I've had details firmed up.' He took out a map, unrolled it before him and stabbed a finger at it. 'That's where the main Lazy Anchor herd is.

So we ride well clear of that, riding north then swinging west. That way the regular crew won't see us. We'll be off trails so nobody else will see us either.'

He moved his finger across the map. 'The beef that our pals in the outfit are cutting out for us will be here. We drive 'em up to there.' He pointed to a spot on the county line.

'How many head?' Dave asked.

'About seventy, give or take.'

'Can we handle a passel that size at night?' Mort asked.

'That's why I've got Johnny as an extra hand,' Wallace said. 'Shouldn't be any problem. The Lazy Anchor boys say there won't be any mavericks or strong-minded bulls amongst them.'

He looked around the gathering. 'Any more questions?'

There were none.

'OK,' he concluded. 'We head out at eleven. Get some shut-eye if you can. And you know my rule — no drinking.

★ ★ ★

With shadows piling up thick they headed out. They travelled silently and swiftly into the deepening night, the only sound: hoofs drumming the ground.

Clouds played peekaboo with the moon so Johnny couldn't see much, but he sensed they were marking out a broad circle rather then heading for their objective in a straight line. Up front, Wallace made a commanding shadow in the darkness. The leader, Johnny had decided, was a competent *hombre* at his task. He would have been an asset to the army: he made decisions without hivering and hovering, and spoke firmly to his men. Not like a lot of shysters who had worn officer's markings.

Eventually Wallace uttered something and the party came to a halt near a dark patch of trees. When the horsemen had gathered round him he spoke in an undertone. 'This is about it by my reckoning. You boys stay here while I go on ahead and check everything's OK. And keep your noise down.'

The men dismounted and watched their leader proceed at a walking pace, horse and rider disappearing into the velvety pall. There was a cattle smell on the night air and in the stillness Johnny could hear occasional muted lowing.

Sometime later Wallace reappeared. 'The brutes are tired,' he said, 'so they'll be easy to handle.' With that he beckoned his men to follow. Momentarily, clouds cleared and in the moonlight Johnny could see a blot of cattle.

He heard faint voices between Wallace and Lazy Anchor crew as final details of the exchange were made.

Anxiety gave orders about positions and Johnny was stationed on flank, presumably where, as the untested new boy, he could do the least damage. He was no sooner in position when the cattle were urged into movement. The shebang hadn't gone very far when a shot, hard and crisp, carried over their heads. Surprised, Johnny looked back but the cattle had reacted to the unexpected noise by stepping up a gear, and he had to fasten his attention on keeping them in check. Then another report echoed across the plains. He dearly wanted to know what was going on but he had his hands full.

In the darkness there could have been trouble with a spooked herd but Wallace had stationed an experienced man up front and the cattle were eventually slowed. Questions dogged Johnny's head but with the task in hand they had to remain unanswered.

Some distance on Wallace lost his bearings temporarily as the moon clouded over for a long spell. But after that there were no further aberrations and they journeyed unhindered across flat country. The cattle had been but a vague mass in the darkness but with the coming of light Johnny figured there were eighty head or more. Not long after dawn they made the pass set as the final rendezvous. Wallace's partners in the deal were waiting and took over management of the exercise without stopping the cows.

Wallace met up with the leader of the receiving gang then rejoined his men who had sat down for a smoke while they waited for him. With light now enough to see, he divvied up the take and the men pocketed their shares.

'What was that shooting at the start?' Johnny asked.

Wallace grunted as he returned his wallet to his pocket. 'Another crew member from the Lazy Anchor turned up unexpected. He wasn't in on the deal so it had to be explained to him.' He laughed, then added, 'The explanation was in lead.'

At that the others laughed. Except Johnny who said, 'There were two shots. Why two?'

'The first one only wounded the critter.'

'He had to be killed?'

'Of course. He'd seen everything.

Besides, having one of 'em dead'll help the other guys in their story that they was jumped. Don't worry, Johnny boy, from what they tell me he was a Yank.'

★ ★ ★

It was well into the morning when they got within sight of town. A mite later than anticipated — Wallace had been out on his estimate of how long the operation would take and it hadn't helped when they'd strayed off their course for a spell. But apart from that they had made good time.

They stopped some distance from the edge of town.

'That was a good night's work, boys,' Wallace said. 'The next job's easy pie too. The one I mentioned. Knocking over a Yankee bank. That's in four days' time.'

Anxiety counted on his fingers and then said, 'That'll be Tuesday, won't it, boss?'

'That's right,' Wallace said. 'So I want to see all of you on Monday morning — sober — so we can fix the details.'

He looked over his team once more. 'OK, boys, you know the drill but I'm still reminding you: split and stagger your entries into town; don't let anybody see you've got a sweated up hoss; and don't take any shut-eye till tonight so nobody figures you been up all night. And I shouldn't have to tell you: don't lash out with your dollars for a day or two. Anybody who gets the law round his neck will have me to contend with as well the badge-toters.'

6

While Johnny spent the morning clearing brush around the cabin and axing stovewood he did a lot of thinking. He'd got sucked into something he didn't cotton to. Robbing carpetbaggers was one thing but killing was another. The more he thought about it the more he came to the conclusion he should cut away from the Wallace outfit. He'd got a bundle of dollars in his pocket. Enough to stake him while he travelled looking for legitimate work.

OK, Wallace had been good to him. And there was Anxiety to think about. He'd been good too and might see Johnny's cutting loose as a slap in the face. But by noon he had decided to take the bull by the horns.

Without telling the old man or his daughter about his decision he made the journey down to the Forty-Five and found Wallace in the bar. 'I got something I'd like to say, Mr Wallace,' he said and nodded towards the rear. 'Maybe it'd be better in the back.'

'Sure,' Wallace said and accompanied his visitor through the saloon.

'Fact is, Mr Wallace,' he said when the door was closed behind him, 'I'm kinda fiddlefooted. I wanna hit the trail.'

'You mean leave Logan?'

'Yes, sir. With pa gone the town ain't got nothing for me.'

'I'm sorry you feel that way, Johnny. You're some good kid. You did well last night. I don't want to lose you.'

'I joined your outfit to get myself a grubstake. Now I got that, ain't nothing stopping me moving on.'

'Don't you think you owe me something for that?'

'Don't get me wrong, Mr Wallace. I'm obliged.'

'Well, Johnny, I think you should honour your obligation.'

Johnny breathed deep. He was always

running into folk who were persuasive with words. 'Fact is there's more to it, Mr Wallace. I don't mind taking from Yankees and scalawags, that sets with me OK, but you didn't say nothing about killing.'

'I told you I needed men with guts. You told me you were no stranger to killing when you had to.'

'Yeah, but I've had a bellyful of slaughter. I ain't gonna be party to killing in peacetime. Even Yankees.'

'That business was unfortunate last night. Wasn't intended. Just a tight spot.'

'Working on the wrong side of the law, tight spots are gonna throw up again.'

Wallace paused. 'OK, tell you what. We'll play it your way. I'll put a rein on the trigger-happy hillbillies in the outfit.'

'I'm still out.'

Wallace became serious. 'You can't.'

'Why not?'

'You know too much.'

As the man said the words, Johnny looked at him with new eyes. The man had a stage-actor handsomeness but for the first time Johnny noted defects: the trace of weakness in the chin and the curve of too-easy sensuality in the lips. 'Listen, Mr Wallace,' he said, 'you offered to help me out. I was looking for some jack to get on my feet. You gave me that with dividends on top. I appreciate that. Hell, I wouldn't talk. Just 'cos the deal ain't what I had in mind don't mean I'm gonna blab about your set-up when I've lit out. We're both Southerners, so we got certain codes. If you knew me, you'd know you have nothing to fear about what I know.'

Wallace nodded. 'It's because I'm getting to know you that I value you as a member of the operation. You can handle yourself and I'd like you to stay on.'

Johnny shook his head. 'Thanks for the compliment but I'm still out.'

'What about Tuesday's business? It's

too late for me to get another man and I need every man I have.'

Johnny breathed deep then said, 'OK. I'll give you that because I promised. As long as there's no killing. But after that caper I hit my own trail.'

★ ★ ★

Before he left town he bought Veener a brooch that took his fancy. A brightly coloured porcelain thing of flowers. He figured, finding herself living in a man's world she needed some acknowledgement she was female. Whether she did or not she was delighted with it and wore it at dinner that night.

After the meal, another splendid offering, he was sitting with Anxiety on the porch as was becoming their regular habit. He was quite tired having spent the bulk of the day on chores; the lean-to serving as a stable was rickety and had needed strengthening. When they were alone with their smokes the old man said, 'Reckon the lassie has taken a shine to you, young man.'

'I think I'm taking a shine to her too, Mr Jones. But it wouldn't be fair for me to make any overtures.'

'Why not? I'd rather it be you keeping her company than some half-brained brush-popper off the plains. Or one of the sleazy lechers holding up a bar in town.'

'I'm only here temporary, you know that.' He had decided against telling the old man of his firm plans yet awhile; for one reason he might try persuading him to stay. He would tell him at the time of leaving. 'It wouldn't be fair to start something which could lead to sadness.'

Anxiety raised his eyebrows. 'Young men have sure changed since my day.'

* * *

It was the next day and Wallace had got the men together in the back room for briefing. Johnny had told

Anxiety nothing about his decision and conversation.

'The best way to knock over a bank is when it's closed,' Wallace was telling the assembled crew. 'That way there ain't any fuss about making a getaway.' He looked at Johnny. 'You don't have to worry about us dealing out lead pills to any bozos who try to stand in our way. That'd set well with you, wouldn't it, Johnny?'

'Sure. But you've still got to plan the getaway mighty careful. Ain't any way I heard of blasting open a safe without waking up everyone in town.'

Wallace smiled. 'If it's timed right we don't have to blast open any safes.' He touched the side of his temple. 'Brains, Johnny boy. That's what this outfit's all about. You gotta time the operation right. What we do is, make our entry into the bank in the early hours and wait for the manager to turn up. Managers arrive well before they open the doors to the public and well before the tellers. A heap of time for us to persuade him to open the safe, load up and leave in a leisurely fashion.'

'What bank you got in mind?'

'The Cattleman's in Cardinal. I've had my eye on it for some time. Cased it proper. It's our kind of bank. Run by Yankee carpetbaggers.'

'How do we mask the noise of breaking in?' Dave asked. 'Sound carries helluva way in a quiet town.'

'Like I said: planning. We don't have to break in. A sidekick of mine in Cardinal has managed to put the squeeze on one of the tellers. Got his gal to get the clerk into a compromising position then bursts in acting the enraged husband. The fellow is a married man and upstanding church-goer. My pardner threatened to beat him up and tell his missus. Once he'd got him sweating he offered him a deal to avoid both. All he'd gotta do was leave a door unlocked. When we leave we smash up the door a mite, make it look like we broke in. That'll take suspicion off the teller and not give him cause to shoot his mouth off.'

He looked around the group. 'Any questions?'

There were none.

'OK,' he said, 'We meet up at the gully near Bluegrass Flats at four this afternoon. Then we'll ride out to a disused line shack that I know of on the way to Cardinal to hole up for the night.'

7

They headed out from the line shack in the early hours of the morning. The place had been musty with disuse and there had been no blankets but several had managed to grab a little sleep; particularly Mort who had moaned grumpily about needing his seven hours when they had eventually roused him.

They made Cardinal in two hours of silent riding through the chill night air. There was no one about as they entered the still dark town. Wallace knew exactly what he was doing and led them to the alleyway at the back of the Cattleman's Bank. He checked the door was unlocked as arranged and the rest dismounted. 'Get your saddle-bags inside in readiness,' Wallace said in a low voice. Optimistic with regard to their haul, he had ordered them to equip themselves with two sets of bags each. 'Lenny, you bring the rope.'

Dave stayed outside on lookout and to watch the horses.

The other four followed Wallace through the building. It was pitch black inside but he knew the layout. After a quick scout round the interior he satisfied himself which room held the safe, then identified a poky little store-room. 'That's where we stick the manager when we've tied him up.' Then he led them all to the front lobby.

Lenny lingered behind, feeling his way along the back of the counter. 'Hey, boss, there's loose change in the cash drawers.'

'Don't bother with the chickenfeed,' Wallace said. 'Too heavy. When the time comes you're gonna have enough to handle with the big stuff. Come on through.'

Lenny reluctantly joined them as they stationed themselves around the room to wait in the darkness. Mort yawned and wanted to smoke to keep himself awake as they whiled away the time; but Wallace forbade it, lest the smell alert the manager before he had fully entered the building. It was silent except for the sound of breathing and the occasional creak of boards as one of them rearranged his position.

Eventually, after what had seemed an interminable wait, dawn began to throw its light through the gaps at the sides of the blinds.

'Shouldn't be long now,' Wallace said. Then: 'Hold the fort, boys. I'm gonna check everything's OK with Dave.'

He made his way outside. Dave was stroking the nose of a horse. 'Things going OK in there, boss?' the handler asked.

'Yeah. Just a matter of waiting. Everything quiet out here?'

'Lenny's horse started nickering but I've quieted him.'

In the gloom Wallace took out his watch and angled it skyward to read the dial. 'Probably another half-hour,' he said and returned inside. On his way back he found the manager's office. He sat in the swivel chair behind the big mahogany desk and patted the arm-rests in silent contemplation. Then began to explore the drawers. In one of the top ones he found a derringer. He hefted it in his hand and was about to check it over when there was a crash from the lobby.

Pushing the derringer into a pocket, he made his way quickly through. 'What's up?' he wanted to know.

'Sorry, boss,' Mort said. He was rubbing his face. 'Dozed off and fell over.'

'You big lunk. You knew what this caper was all about. You should have got whatever sleep you needed well before. Now, pull yourself together.'

Then he instructed them to pull their bandannas over their faces and reminded them not to use names once the heist was under way. Another step nearer action the men resumed their statuesque positions.

Wallace stood behind the door. The strengthening shafts of light caught dust motes and occasionally they would hear horses or a wagon roll by as the town began to come to life. From time to time Wallace would look through the chink of a blind without moving it. They tensed in anticipation each time the sound of footsteps reached them, then relaxed a shade as the sound faded; but always in a condition of readiness.

Lenny was standing against the front wall where he could be seen from the door should it be opened. Wallace gestured to catch his attention. 'Get further back so you can't be seen,' he whispered. Lenny backed accordingly.

Now there was sufficient light Wallace looked regularly at his watch. Finally, distinct footsteps on the boards outside. Then the chinking of keys. The acceleration of events pumped adrenalin through Johnny's body. Having waited for so long he had adjusted to inactivity.

The door opened, dazzling light cascaded through, and a figure appeared in the doorway. The man entered and turned to close the door; his face, momentarily caught in the sun, illustrated the preoccupation with routine. But all that changed as Wallace's gun barrel stuck in his neck during the action of closing the door.

'Don't make a noise,' the leader said, 'and your missus won't be a widow this day.'

The man's face blanched, his eyes filled with terror. When he whimpered 'Don't hurt me, mister' Wallace knew things were going to run smooth.

'You're gonna be gagged.' Wallace told him, taking a piece of rawhide from his jacket pocket and throwing it to Lenny. 'Then you're gonna take us through to the safe and open it. No problems, no rumpus, no nothing. OK?'

The man nodded.

'Right.' Wallace instructed Johnny to keep guard by the door and Lenny lodged the rawhide through the mouth of the bank man, tying it at the back. Then the man was nudged towards the walkway through the counter. When the group reached the room harbouring the safe, Wallace told one of them to light the oil-lamp.

It was a modern safe with thick door but having the keys made it as vulnerable as a child's tin money-box. The door swinging open elicited gasps from the onlookers: the box was chock full.

'All good Union currency,' Wallace grunted as he hefted one of the many wads of bills. 'Now you can see why we don't bother with coins.' He indicated Mort. 'Now you tie the bozo up good and proper and get him into that store-room where he can't hear or see nothing. You other two help me start stashing the loot. Only take bills and certificates. Pay no mind to documents and other stuff. We can't use 'em.'

As soon as the first two sets of bags were filled Wallace said to Anxiety,

'Take these out to Dave. They're his. Tell him to stand by. As soon as we've got a couple more filled, I want the boys to start moving out at staggered intervals. Say a minute's break between each. Leaving singly with good gaps between us will reduce the chances of attracting attention.'

Shortly there were only Wallace and Johnny left in the building. Wallace carried his own bulging bags to the back. Outside Mort was alone standing beside the remaining three horses.

'Now git,' Wallace said, as he slung the bags over his horse. 'And keep it quiet.'

Mort mounted and leant forward. 'You be OK, boss?'

'Sure. Just gotta fetch Johnny.'

As Mort headed out Wallace returned inside. He put his head through the back door of the lobby. 'OK, Johnny, come and get your bags. Let's make tracks.'

He stood behind the door and as Johnny came through he clubbed him on the head. The young man collapsed.

Wallace had thought it all out beforehand. Even though the manager hadn't heard any names or seen them unmasked there was always the chance of him giving the law some clue. When he had cased the place he had noted that Cardinal was the site of an office for the newly formed state police: and it would be them who would be on this caper. Wallace didn't know their potential. They were untried. But one thing he did know: they would be out to prove themselves in front of the other law agencies who would be only too ready to see the new boys fall flat on their faces.

Second, he couldn't have Faldeau walking out on him like he was planning. Despite what the ex-Confederate had said the gang boss couldn't trust him not to blab. Besides, nobody walked out on Henry P. Wallace. What he had in mind would solve both problems.

Wallace leant over the Texan and gave him another with the gun butt across the side of the temple to make sure. Then he hauled his still form along the corridor till they were outside the store-room. Anxious to contain as much sound as possible, he moved swiftly round the interior of the building, closing all open doors. From the washroom he took a towel which he wrapped round his gun, enveloping chamber, barrel and muzzle. He opened the door of the store-room and entered. Mort had done a good job; the bank man was utterly transfixed by his binding.

There were were no windows so when Wallace closed the door of the store-room for extra muffling he hoped the prostrate manager wouldn't shift position. He acted quickly just in case and put the gun against the bank manager's forehead. He pulled the trigger and flung open the door, choking on the cordite fumes.

Confused and facing bright light from utter darkness the manager had not had time to attempt any movement and the shot was well placed.

Intending to use the derringer on Faldeau, Wallace began unravelling his own pistol in order to holster it. However, the barrel now protruded through a blackened hole making separation of the two items awkward for a man in a hurry; and, in trying to extricate it from the towel he dropped the weapon. Cursing and leaving it where it was he took out the derringer. He levelled it inches away from Johnny's head and pulled the trigger. But the action elicited nothing more than a dull click. Wasn't loaded!

Hell, he remembered he had been in the act of checking it for loads when Mort had distracted him by causing the noise in the lobby. Then other matters had taken over his thoughts and he'd completely forgotten about the damn thing. There was a box of rounds in the manager's office but there was no time for traipsing back there.

He retrieved his own gun from the

boards, aimed that at Johnny's head and tried to thumb the hammer. He couldn't. He held the gun by the barrel to give himself more leverage and tried again. Stiffly the hammer moved back, but only a fraction, then no more. He looked at it in the half light and fiddled with it. Nothing doing. When he had dropped it a few moments before, the hammer mechanism had been knocked out of line within the frame. He cursed himself for his choice of weapon. Single-frame jobs you could mishandle for a month of Sundays but a Colt was delicate. One bang on the ground could be enough to dislodge the components, requiring reassembly before it was operable.

He glanced at the prone Johnny. He'd given him two blows to the head, the second savage and deliberately aimed. Maybe the bozo was pegging out now.

He'd wanted him dead but there was nothing more he could do about the situation apart from skedaddling.

The first report had been muffled but probably had been enough to alert somebody. He had to move to save his own skin.

He laid the useless pistol near the Texan's still hand and took a final glance at the scene. He could see the bank manager in the store-room still tied up. He undid the knots, cast the rope aside and kicked the derringer towards the man. Then he grabbed the remaining bags and loped outside.

There was still no one about. Something to be thankful for: not all his luck had gone down the privy. He freed Johnny's horse and tapped its rump. Then he untethered his own horse, heaved himself into the saddle. Nudging his mount into an unhurried gait down the alley, he left as quietly as he had ridden in.

★ ★ ★

The four were waiting in the lee of a stand of trees some miles out of

Cardinal when Wallace rejoined them, laden down with four sets of bags.

'Where's Johnny?' Anxiety asked, looking down the leader's backtrail.

'Bad news. There was some shooting.'

'Things were going so well,' Dave said.

'We got the law on our tail?' Mort wanted to know.

'Ain't see'd none yet but they'll be coming.'

Anxiety was still concerned about the young men. 'You telling us we've lost Johnny?' he pressed.

'Seems that way,' Wallace said, throwing one of the sets of encumbering bags to Lenny who was nearest. 'Here, look after that.'

Unlike the others Anxiety was not looking back in the direction of Cardinal. He was still staring at his boss. 'What do you mean — seems?'

'Look,' Wallace said impatiently. 'It happened. I was with the horses. I heard shooting. I dashed back inside. The bank guy had got free and got a derringer from somewhere. The two of them were on the floor. They were both covered with blood. The old man was certainly dead.'

'Johnny hadn't got a gun.'

'I'd handed him mine while I'd gone out to the horses.'

'Let's git,' Mort said in agitation.

'Hold your horses,' Anxiety snapped. 'How many shots were there?'

'Two or three. I don't know. It all happened so quick.' Wallace didn't like the way the conversation was going. One thing he didn't want was his men thinking he was partial to getting rid of one of their number. Once that suspicion got a toehold a guy might wonder if he would be next; then he couldn't trust nobody. 'Mort's right, let's move.'

They gigged their horses and headed out from cover.

Once they were under way Anxiety drew alongside Wallace. 'Was Johnny hit? Did you see him?'

'He seemed in a bad way. Like I

said, there was blood.'

'Didn't you try to get him out?' Anxiety shouted against the gathering slipstream.

'I couldn't move him quick enough. I was struggling with him when I heard somebody coming. Had to get the hell out myself.'

'I thought you said you didn't know if we was being trailed.'

'Takes time to raise a posse.'

Mort was catching snippets of the conversation. 'How did the bank guy get free? I trussed him up like a turkey cock.'

'You were half asleep, you bozo,' Wallace yelled, urging his horse faster. 'You fouled up tying the critter up.'

'Hell, no I didn't, Mr Wallace.'

'Hell, yes. You'd already fallen asleep on the job. Tell you one thing: that happens again and you're out of the outfit.'

'Like Johnny,' Anxiety muttered under his breath.

8

Things wobbled into focus. A ceiling. Then walls. The bank; he was still in the bank. He felt a draught cutting through the corridor. An outside door was open. But most of all he was aware of a throbbing head. He heaved himself onto his elbows. The bank manager was lying half out of the store-room. He had no forehead. Just a bloody caved-in hole. What the hell had happened? One minute he had been all set to leave, the next — wham.

Events rushed back. He'd been coming from where he'd been guarding the door in the lobby and he'd got hit on the back of the head. Couldn't have been the bank man. He'd been securely tied up. Mort had seen to that.

Had the gang been surprised by someone? He reckoned not. He saw the derringer. Where the hell had that come from? And a Colt. He picked it up. The hammer was obviously jammed.

He hauled himself to his feet, the effort sending throbbing pulses through his head. Jeez. It wasn't just the back of his skull; there was pain exploding like red hell through the side of his temple. He gingerly probed with fingers. He could feel the lump rising.

And where were the boys? He staggered towards the back door. Maybe the last was waiting for him. Wallace or Lenny. On his way he paused at the door of the deposit room. No saddle-bags, no money, no boys. Zilch.

He breathed deeply, trying to pull himself and his thoughts together. While he was doing so he heard footsteps. But they were coming from the front lobby. Feet clattering on boards. He staggered in their direction expecting to see one of the boys. Then there was a voice shouting 'Mr Shawcroft?' and, instead of one of the gang members, he came face to face with a young man in a tight-fitting suit, peering hesitantly into the corridor.

'Holy Moses,' the man exclaimed and turned tail. Johnny heard him exiting out front.

The boys had gone. That was for sure. Time had passed and he was in schtuck. He dropped the gun and staggered out back. No horses. Nothing. Again zilch.

He lurched down the alleyway. The game was up. He had to hide or get away. He couldn't hide forever, not in an unfamiliar town. Must find a horse. Must get the hell out Cardinal.

Before he made it to the open street he found himself at the back of a large building. A small sign gave somebody's name but all that registered was the word 'Livery'. There was a door. He opened it; the welcome whiff of horses and feed hit his nostrils. He crossed the straw-strewn floor to a stall. Beyond the gate a horse stomped its hooves at his approach.

Still dazed he fumbled at the latch. That was as far as he got.

'You make another move, mister, and you've got this pitchfork through your back.'

The statement was illustrated by sharp prongs that he felt in his shoulder blades.

'OK, OK,' he whispered. He turned. One man was levelling the pitchfork at him, another one was advancing with an uplifted hammer. Johnny raised his hands. He wasn't in a fit state to take either of them on.

* * *

'Get that wire to all agencies. State, federal and local. Pronto.'

'Yes, sir.'

With that L. J. Brahms stepped out of the telegraph office. He was irritated. He had a cleaned-out bank on his hands; a bank manager stretched out in the funeral parlour; and a critter in his cell who wouldn't say anything.

The normal procedure was to send out a posse. He'd handled a bank heist once during his days as a town sheriff but there were two things that stymied that action in this case. First, he was now with the state police and they were not empowered to raise posses. Second, nobody had seen the robbers leave town so he didn't know which way to start searching. And the one in the hoosegow was plain muleheaded in his refusal to say anything. The only thing going in his favour so far was at least he'd got one of the varmints behind bars whether he would sing or not.

He made his way back to the office. There was a small crowd outside being held at bay by one of the troopers.

'It true you got Dan Shawcroft's killer?' an angry onlooker asked.

'I got somebody in custody,' the police chief answered. 'But who killed who's gotta be sorted out in court.'

'Thought I'd better keep watch outside,' the trooper said. 'They were making a nuisance of themselves trying to get in.'

The chief patted the arm of the guard. 'Good man, Lyle. You're right. Better stay here a spell.'

'Hear tell he was caught red-handed,' the vocal onlooker persisted.

'Ain't no reason to waste money on no trial,' another shouted to accompanying cheers.

Brahms paused with his hand on the doorknob. 'Due process of law, you know that.'

Inside an elderly gent in a dark suit was waiting for him. Further back a young subordinate officer was pouring out coffee.

'Ah, you got the message,' the police captain said, noting his visitor. 'Glad to see you, Seth.'

The man nodded. 'Came as soon as I heard, LJ. Poor old Shawcroft.'

'Yeah. Wouldn't hurt a fly.' Brahms went to the window and looked over the half-curtain at the crowd. 'Damn idlers. Got nothing better to do.'

'What you got, LJ?' the elder man asked.

The captain dropped his hat on a stand and settled into his chair behind the desk. 'It was well planned. Looks they must have gained entry before dawn and lay waiting for Shawcroft.'

'How'd they get in?'

'Lock's broke at the back.'

'Orlando here tells me you got no idea where they vamoosed.'

The young officer nodded an endorsement at the mention of his name.

'That's the hell of it,' Brahms went on. 'Crept into town and crept out again. Nobody seen hide nor hair of 'em. Don't even know how many varmints were in the caper. Must have been a few though. Shawcroft's teller says that the safe was full. You'd need a few horses to freight that out.'

'Unless they used a wagon.'

'Maybe. But I doubt it. A wagon doesn't move quick enough. And they'd know all wagons on the trails within fifty miles would be searched within hours of the news getting out.'

'Maybe they're local.'

Brahms thumbed towards the cell. 'He ain't local.'

'Where's he from?'

'Don't know. But don't recognize him as local. Can't get nothing out of him. Won't say nothing about who was riding with him. Huh, honour amongst thieves.'

From his cell Johnny heard the words and pondered on them. Honour amongst thieves. In a way the police chief was right. Although this was to have been his last caper, and he didn't trust Wallace as far as he could throw him, he still wouldn't sing. He had no reason to cause harm to the other guys in the outfit. He didn't like them, but that was no reason to play canary on them. And there was no way he would finger Anxiety. He was the big stumbling block. He'd been a friend of his father, had helped him; and had been kind to Johnny himself, even being instrumental in getting him into Wallace's outfit. It hadn't turned out right from the start; but Anxiety had only been trying to help him.

'Let's have coffee here, Orlando,' Brahms said before resuming the discourse with his visitor. 'I'm getting Harris from the photograph parlour to take a picture of him. When that's been circulated we might get some idea of which neck of the woods the jasper has crawled out of.'

The man from the back handed him a tin mug of steaming coffee. The chief took a sip and went on, 'The quicker this is off my hands the better.' He raised a hand towards the other officer. 'Orlando, close that door.'

The trooper closed the door that separated the cells and office. Confident that the prisoner couldn't overhear, Brahms continued in a lowered voice. 'I figure it's a big gang, Seth. Big enough to try springing him. I'm short-staffed. I've only got four men. One's down sick and another's got compassionate leave, mother's funeral in Louisiana. So won't be back for quite a spell. That leaves me, Lyle and Orlando. So the sooner this thing is off our books the better. It's a cut-and-dried case.'

'I don't think it is cut and dried, sir,' said Orlando pulling up a chair and joining them at the desk. He was young, looked barely out of his teens, while his Northern-toned voice offered a strong contrast against the Texan drawls of the others.

'No?' the man called Seth queried. 'Why not?'

'The guy we got back there wasn't toting a holster.'

'He could have brung the gun tucked into his belt,' the police chief countered. 'Some guys do that.'

The trooper shook his head. 'Lodged in a belt isn't the wisest way to carry a weapon on a long ride, sir. Especially if you might have some dashing around to do, like you might expect knocking over a bank.'

'I see,' Seth said.

'And another thing,' the trooper went on. 'Mr Shawcroft was an old man.

111

Not entirely your energetic type. Don't think he could have inflicted bruises like that on a young man.'

'Could if he surprised him,' Brahms chipped in.

'Well if he surprised him, what was that rope doing there?' Orlando retorted.

There was reproach in Captain Brahms's eyes as he looked at Trooper Orlando Shepherd. 'Forget all that,' he said irritatedly. 'Anyways, boy, what do you know about these things?'

At that, the noise level outside rose and the door opened. It was the telegraph operator. 'Can't get your messages through, Mr Brahms. Wire must be down.'

'You mean there's no way of getting messages out?'

'Not through my office.'

'Hell's teeth,' the chief mouthed. 'How long's it been dead?'

'Can't say. Yours has been the first message I've tried to send out since yesterday noon. Could have happened anytime since then.'

'So we don't know whether these varmints have cut the wire or it's happened by accident.'

'Right.'

'How you gonna find out what the trouble is?'

'Well, I'll wait for a spell because the fault could be at the other end. Happens from time to time. If it isn't activated in a couple of hours I'll ride out and check the line myself. See if I can find the break.'

'How long we talking about?'

'Could take a day.'

Brahms snorted then waved a dismissive hand to the operator who came back with 'Sorry, Captain Brahms. I'll let you know when the fault's found and it's been reconnected.'

Brahms accompanied him as he left. Outside, the police chief watched the operator having to force his way through the enlarged crowd. He raised his arms. 'Now listen, folks. There ain't no developments happening here.

There's nothing to see. So just go about your affairs.'

No one moved so he continued in a lowered voice, 'I know how you feel but I got a job to do and it ain't helped none by having you lot blocking up the coming and going. So, please do as I ask.'

One moved, then another. When the immediate boardwalk was clear he thumbed to the trooper to follow him.

Inside he said, 'Lyle, I've just heard the telegraph is down. It's important we get word to all the relevant agencies. I want you to collect the messages that I've left in the operator's office and take them to Westering. That's the nearest place with a telegraph. Make sure they get through. It'll be the best part of two days there and back. So say goodbye to your missus but put some haste into it.'

The trooper saluted. 'Yes, sir.'

As he left the mayor rose. 'I gotta be going too.'

'Do me a favour, Seth.'

'Sure.'

'Judge's in session at the moment. You go past the court building, don't you? Ask him to stop by here as soon as he's finished.'

'Sure, LJ.'

★ ★ ★

It was nearly noon and a crowd was building up in front of the office again. Brahms had been joined by the judge and mayor and had just put the court man in the picture. 'So you can see, Abe, I'm in a spot here. Don't know how long I can hold back the townsfolk. I want things moving as soon as possible. What's the soonest you can arrange for the trial?'

The elderly man shook his head. 'Can't handle it, LJ.'

'Hell, why not? You're the judge for these parts.'

'Things have changed, LJ. Can't handle murder no more. Trial has to be held in Austin. State matter.'

It took a moment for the information to register then Brahms rubbed his chin. 'Can't the trial be delegated to the local level, then we can hold it right here in town?'

'LJ, you've not been reading the small print in the documents they put out. There's a new scheme of things. Reconstruction they call it.' He grunted. 'The very job you've got is part of the new set up. You know that.'

That was true and Brahms had been glad to get it. The newly created job had its problems: sandwiched in between local and federal law, the state police was the new boy on the block and the older agencies weren't in the frame of mind for co-operating.

'That's right, LJ,' the mayor endorsed. 'This Reconstruction thing is rejigging all legal and political set-ups.'

Brahms waved at the door. 'Orlando, get your ass down to Harris's photograph parlour. Tell him to bring his contraption round here. I got a picture I want taking.'

He waited until the trooper disappeared. 'Listen. I'm down to two men already. Then this morning I've had to send Lyle out to Westering to get messages to all the authorities. So, there's only me and Orlando in the damn place. I can't escort the prisoner and leave a Northerner in charge of the state police office. You know what folks think about Yankees, see 'em all as carpetbaggers. There'd be hell to pay.'

The other nodded. 'I agree, local feelings wouldn't hold with that. Him being a young greenhorn to boot, they'd make his life hell before you got back. Probably torch the place to the ground.'

'What the bee-jesus do I do, Abe?'

'Nothing for it. Send Orlando with the prisoner.'

'All the way to Austin? A Yankee towing a Southerner in irons?'

'I figure you're gonna have to, LJ. No option. The only alternative is to hold the prisoner here indefinitely. Shawcroft was a respected man. There's a heap of ugly feeling amongst the citizenry out there about the fellow you got back in the cell. There's a passel of 'em outside now.'

'I know. I've dispersed 'em once already. Keeping 'em away is like trying to keep flies off a dung heap.'

'Wouldn't take many more to break him out and lynch him. Not with just you and a fancy-talking Northerner standing in the way. If it takes Lyle two days, you've got at least one long night to get through. Could be nasty when the saloons close.'

Brahms pondered on it. 'State police has been going for six months. Ain't ever heard of troopers losing a prisoner to a lynch mob yet — and I don't aim to be the first.'

'Then you got no option. One way or another you've got to get him to Austin pending trial. Seems the only course open is using the Northerner. Maybe it's about time you gave him something to do other than coffee making.'

Minutes later there was a commotion outside and the young trooper

118

reappeared. 'They're getting ugly-faced out there, sir,' he said as he closed the door, shutting out the noise behind him. 'Some are carrying pick handles now.'

Brahms checked through the window again. 'Jeez.'

'Mr Harris says he'll be along directly,' the trooper went on. 'Just has to prepare plates or something.'

'OK,' Brahms said, turning from the window, 'when that's done with I'm giving you a job, Orlando. An important job. You're to escort the prisoner to Austin.'

Knowing his boss's attitude to his youth and origins the man was taken aback but very quickly gave a positive, 'Yes, sir.'

'You've got to leave as soon as possible. I'll draw up some documentation and give you the address in Austin.'

'Ain't never been to Austin before, sir.'

Brahms shook his head in resignation.

'If I had another guy, I'd send him. Look on this as an education. Come here, boy.' He took the trooper to the map on the wall and studied it, placing his finger on Cardinal. 'You can read, can't you?'

'Yes, sir.'

'That's a blessing,' the chief said in exaggerated relief as he swung his finger upwards. 'Well, reckon the best way is ride north till you reach the Texas and Arizona Rail Road. See, here at Sand Creek. Then take the train into Austin.'

The young man absorbed the information, then said, 'Ain't never been on a train before, sir.'

The police chief rolled his eyes, looking back at the judge and unspoken words passed between them. To Orlando he said, 'You sure you can handle this?'

The Northerner saluted. 'Yes, indeed, sir.'

'That's good — because you've got to, Trooper. Now, I'll give you some dough out of the petty cash. You'll have to buy some accommodation along the way and in Austin.'

He moved away from the map. 'OK. When the time comes the judge and I'll disperse those bozos outside. Don't think I can keep 'em away indefinite but enough so that you and the prisoner can slip out back.' He returned to his desk. 'Come on, Abe. Help me draw up the documents.'

9

Saddle-bags bulging with stores, Orlando led his prisoner out of town. Soon brush gave way to open country and they pushed on across the plains. They rode steady and silently. With handcuffs restricting his movement, Johnny brooded on the situation: not only being taken in for a killing he hadn't done but the indignity of being in the custody of a damn Yankee. Hell, he couldn't see how the State of Texas could put a badge on a Northerner. One thing he knew: it wasn't going to end like this. He would have a go at jumping this fellow when the time was right. His brawl in the saloon had proved to him that, despite his crook leg, he could still handle himself.

Noon found them pushing up a grade and, at the crest, Orlando noted a shallow dip rimmed by greenery ahead. 'We'll noon down there,' he said. 'There'll be water and shade too.' They wended their way down to the creek and he called a halt near some trees.

Giving the order to dismount, he took the horses for a brief drink at the seep before unsaddling them and groundhitching them to graze.

'Hope you like beans,' he said as he opened up a saddle-bag.

'I've ate worse,' Johnny said, taking off his campaign hat. He skimmed it to the ground and wiped his brow as best he could with cuffed hands. Bringing up the rear he had had little chance to study his captor. He watched the man as he set about building a fire and preparing the meal. The down on the young face looked as though it had not yet seen a razor. And that Yankee way of talking. Johnny had fought to keep these folks' noses out of Southern affairs; and now the big hats were putting stars on their shirts. He wondered what it had all been for.

When he was ready to dole out the fare Orlando hefted up a saddle and dropped it near Johnny. 'Don't want no trouble,' he said. 'You understand?' He waited until he received a resentful nod of acquiescence then took the key from his pocket and, guardedly, undid one of the cuffs, fixing it to the saddle horn.

With Johnny once again secured the trooper returned to the fire and spooned out portions of beans.

'I didn't kill that man, you know,' Johnny said, as the young trooper handed him his plate and a hunk of bread.

'Ain't up to me to do any judging,' Orlando said, settling down to eat. 'That's up to the authorities in Austin. I got a job to do is all. Now that's good food, get yourself around it. Don't know when we'll be spelling again.'

Johnny delved into the beans and they continued their meal in silence. As he finished and wiped bread round the plate he said, 'I was with a gang knocking off the bank, sure, but I didn't shoot nobody.'

The other took the plate from him. 'When we get to Austin it might help your case if you give the names of the other gang members.'

Johnny thought on it as the trooper set to preparing coffee. Just as he'd thought on it ever since they'd slapped him behind bars. Wallace had framed him and he could give his name. Seemed crazy that he didn't. Might have to eventually. But Anxiety was the stumbling block. It just didn't set well with Johnny to incriminate him. He was sure the oldster had had nothing to do with framing him. He'd been a good friend to him and his pa. He recalled how the man had seen his pa through illness when he come down with fever. If Johnny was to give names, he had to get back to Logan and warn Anxiety so that he could light out before the manure started flying. Or get word to him somehow. With Anxiety clear, he would be free to give names.

'Sure don't understand why you

don't come clean,' Orlando continued as he handed his prisoner a tin mug of coffee. 'Whatever the truth is, that way what's right should come out.'

Johnny shook his head. 'Can't do that.'

And that was the end of that particular exchange. He took out the makings. 'I got time for a smoke?'

'Sure,' Orlando said. He stood up and moved around starting the business of tidying up. In the process he picked up the prisoner's campaign hat with the intention of throwing it closer to the man but he noticed something protruding slightly from the sweatband inside. He extracted it to discover it was a piece of paper. He unfolded it. 'What do you know,' he said. 'Your army paper.'

'Hey, that's private,' the other said, making a move to stand up and retrieve it.

'Stay where you are,' Orlando warned. 'You gave up the notion of having private things when you knocked over

126

the Cardinal Bank.'

Noting the trooper was already reading the few words inscribed on the document, Johnny realized there was nothing he could do about it now, so resumed his cigarette building.

'So you do have a name,' Orlando observed with some triumph in his voice. 'John . . . ' He stopped, considered, then read the surname slowly, syllable by painful syllable. 'Fald-ee-aw — that how you say it?'

Johnny smirked at the result. 'You're the one who's claiming to be able to read.'

The trooper continued with the rest of the document which presented less of a problem. 'Attached to Troop C, Second Texas. Volunteer. Made corporal. Good war record too. Commendations.'

'I did my bit.'

'Says here your home town's Logan. I heard of that. So that's where you hail from, eh?'

Johnny realized the damage had been done so he did his best to dismiss it. 'Long time ago,' he said casually. 'Ain't been back since the war though. Nothing to go back to. Folks are long dead. Dunno what the place looks like now.'

Orlando read through the document once more, then passed it over together with the hat. 'At least we've got a label for you now.'

Johnny folded up the document, returned it to the inside of the hat and set it back on his head. He finished his drink, threw the dregs away. 'Nature calls,' he said, as he handed back the mug.

'OK,' the trooper said, 'do what you have to. But remember, Johnny — no tricks.' He released the cuff from the saddle horn. Johnny rose and walked away a few paces.

Orlando resumed tidying up, glancing back to watch Johnny return after he had relieved himself. 'Where'd you get the crook leg?' he asked as he indicated for his prisoner's wrists to be presented once more.

'Richmond.'

'You had a bad war then?'

'Bad enough. We lost.'

Orlando nodded and clicked the cuff secure. 'And the bad times ain't over.'

Johnny grunted in endorsement of the sentiment. 'You sure right there, boy.'

Then Orlando attended to his own ablutions and they mounted up.

* * *

A little further on they passed some workers in a field. Then the trail wended through bleaker terrain. Less vegetation, fewer trees, no habitations, no people. There was little to take the eye unless you found rock formations interesting. Once Johnny noted three riders limned on the western ridge, heading in the same direction. He saw Orlando's head turn and take note of them. He didn't know how long they'd been there but they didn't break the monotony for long, disappearing as suddenly as they had appeared.

'Don't you ever speak?' Johnny asked after a long spell with nothing to listen to but the crunch of hooves.

'Only when I got something to say.'

And that was the end of that conversation.

Orlando continued to push the horses across empty, sun-scorched land. Johnny's eyes were closing, his head dropping forward, when a booming voice brought the small train to a halt.

'Well, what have we here?'

Johnny roused and looked ahead. They had just rounded a rough cluster of tall rock forcing a bend in the trail and had come face to face with three riders blocking the path. Had to be the three gents he had seen earlier. So that was it. They'd been dogging the pair.

'Howdy,' Orlando said.

The leader, older than his companions, had a broad peasant face decorated by bushy sideburns. He nodded his head. 'That ain't a badge, is it?'

Orlando stiffened. 'It is. And the man behind it is asking you step aside, sir.'

The man laughed and looked at his comrades who were leaning over their saddle horns. 'Well, there's a Yankee talking if ever I heard one.' His gaze moved to the prisoner. 'You a Northerner too?'

Johnny shook his head. 'The hell I am. Texas born and bred.'

The questioner's look returned to the trooper. 'And how come a badge gets pinned to the chest of a young Stars-and-Striper like you, sonny?'

'The same way it gets pinned to a southern one. I'm a state-commissioned officer going about his lawful business and I'm asking you once more to allow me to pass.'

The sideburned one serioused up. 'I don't like lawmen at the best of times, boy, but the notion of a Yankee claiming to have jurisdiction in Texas

— now that real sticks in my craw.' He spat into the trail dust. 'And clapping irons on a Southern boy.'

Orlando drew his gun. 'I don't want no trouble.'

The man laughed humourlessly. 'Now that's a real foolish thing to do, son. If you're lucky you might hit me. But sure as hell there'll be three slugs in your Yankee hide. Take the gun, Zeke.'

One of the younger men dismounted slowly and walked to the side so he could approach Orlando at an angle. Up close he reached out. Orlando moved the gun away, still keeping it level, paused then allowed the man called Zeke to take it.

'That's better,' the old man said. 'More civilized. If a carpetbagger like you knows what that word means. Now get down and give us the key to those irons.'

Orlando complied. His gunrig was removed and he was told to go sit near a sun-bleached tree. Seconds later

Johnny was rubbing his freed wrists.

'What you got took for?' one of the trio asked.

The liberated prisoner was about to give some explanation but the leader stepped in. 'Ain't none of our business, boys, and we don't want to know. We ain't no jury. Don't like seeing Yankees being uppity in our neck of the woods is all.'

'What we gonna do with the feller, boss? Have some fun?'

'Nope. We done what is right is all. And we got a gun and a hoss out of it for our pains.'

He walked across to Orlando, leant forward and ripped the badge from the lawman's shirt. He pondered on it as he weighed it in his hand. 'This is small-town Texas country, son. A place where bleeding heart philosophies ain't held in high regard. I knows you don't think it but we done you a favour. There's are a lotta folks around here lost kinfolk in the war. They come across you like we did and you'd be

133

swinging from this tree you're sitting under. Now git.'

Orlando rose and gave Johnny a look which said 'This isn't the end of it'.

The two younger bushwhackers grinned as they watched the man start to walk back in the direction of Cardinal. Then they took out their guns and loosed off shots that spumed up dirt near Orlando's receding feet. The lawman flinched at the first one, then maintained an unperturbed straight line.

Like his erstwhile prisoner, Orlando had been a soldier. His federal unit had been advancing into Texas at the cessation of hostilities. He had never seen a country so vast and had reckoned it a fitting place in which to start a new life, a state big enough for everybody.

Big enough for everybody? He was beginning to learn that a heap of folk didn't think so.

The young gunnies laughed until their chambers were empty and their little game was over.

When the trooper was a distant figure, the old man turned to Johnny. 'What you gonna do now, pilgrim? Get outa State?'

'Nope. Lie low for a spell — there's a lot of high plains a man can get lost in — then, when things are quieted, I got me some wrongs to right.'

'Well like I said, your business is your business.'

Johnny took the reins of his horse. 'I'm obliged.'

10

Time dragged slowly as Orlando plodded wearily along the trail. In the heat, flies dogged him relentlessly, buzzing round his head. The notion of failure and now exhaustion ate into his brain. He'd been cock-a-hoop at getting the trooper's job. For the first time in his life it had looked like he was getting someplace. If his old pa had been alive he wouldn't have believed seeing his son with a star on his chest. And now he had let everyone down: himself, his pa, his family. Looked like his chance to get out and make something of himself was all over — before it had begun. He had stumbled under the first burden of responsibility that had been put on his shoulders. He knew for sure Captain L. J. Brahms would want to see the back of him.

It was late afternoon when he passed

the workers in the fields he had seen earlier.

'Hi, brother,' one shouted as he loaded corn onto an ox-cart. He was an old man with white hair and a wizened face that reminded Orlando of his father.

Orlando left the trail, grabbing at a chance to make a break in his journey, and joined the man.

'Howdy,' he said, leaning against the wagon and wiping his brow.

The old man paused in his task and looked the traveller over. 'You look bushed.'

'You can say that again.'

'Say, you the feller who was riding north a spell back?'

'On the button. That was me.'

'What's happened to your partner? And where's your horse?'

'That wasn't my partner and I've lost my horse.'

'How come?'

'Fact is, I'm a state trooper and that man was my prisoner.'

The man looked at him quizzically. 'What state you hail from, son?'

'Vermont. You're from the other side of the line too, ain't you?'

'Sure thing. Massachusetts. A couple of families of us moved down when we read of land being available under the Reconstruction programme.' He glanced around. 'Trouble is folks in these parts don't take too kindly to us. Had our crops burnt more than once. They damn anybody with Yankee talk as a carpetbagger.'

'I'm finding that out too,' Orlando added. 'Got jumped by some Texas rednecks. They set my prisoner free and stole my horse and trappings.'

The farm worker became serious. 'Well, what's this state police, you're talking of? Ain't ever heard of it.'

'The top brass figured a new force was necessary because of the breakdown in law and order across the state since the war. Sounds like you know something of these problems.'

The other nodded. 'Say, we're

finishing up here now. If you're in trouble and have a mind, you're welcome to trail with us back to the bunkhouse and share a bite to eat. That is if you don't mind eating with humble field hands.'

Orlando wiped more beads of moisture from his brow. 'Before I joined the bluelegs I was field hand back in Vermont.' He looked down and fingered the rip in his shirt where his badge had been wrenched away. 'And the way this caper is panning out I'll soon be back to hoeing, planting and fattening hogs myself.'

★ ★ ★

It was evening. In the workers' shack Orlando was treated to melon, corn meal and a nibble of chicken while his hosts listened pop-eyed to his tale.

'Imagine us,' one grinned, 'sitting at a table breaking bread with a policeman.'

After a helping of apple pie, the

oldster looked around the gathering. 'Well, if we can't help a fellow Northerner who's making good in a Southern world then we ain't worth our salt. That right, brothers?'

There were sounds of approval.

'OK, we can lend you a horse,' the man continued. 'But times are not good for us so you're obliged to get the creature back to us as soon as you can, son.'

'Of course,' Orlando said. 'Dunno what to say. You've been mighty kind already.'

'OK, that's settled. Well, it's too dark to travel now and you must be tired, so you bunk up with us tonight and light out whenever you've rested up enough.'

Orlando nodded.

'And then what are your plans?' the old man asked, pouring out some juice.

'Report back to Cardinal. The captain is gonna explode over this. He don't lay much store by my capabilities.

Then, when he's calmed down I'll request permission to light out after the fugitive.'

'You'll be coming back this way then?'

'If the boss gives the go-ahead.' He shook his head. 'But just don't know how he's gonna take the news of me losing my man.'

'Well, if you do find yourself heading back out this way, call in on us, brother. We might have information for you.' He winked. 'We Yankees have our own telegraph, just like the local folk. We visit markets and talk with our own kind. We don't say much but we got cyes. Big eyes. You give us a description of this renegade and we'll spread the word about him. Might be able to give you a lead to the direction your feller's heading in.'

'That'd sure be a help. And I'll return your horse at the same time.'

As he spoke he held his hands out to the fire. Meanwhile, many miles out on the high plains, a man was curled up in a hollow.

Hungry and cold, his consolation was he was free.

* * *

The next day found Johnny even hungrier. His morning's travelling was wearisome but the sun at its zenith was to mark some change in fortune. He came upon a round-up crew taking their noon break and camp-fire hospitality saw to it he had a full belly.

* * *

Orlando stopped outside the door of the state police office. He breathed deep, then pushed open the door.

L. J. Brahms was seated at his desk and there was pleasant surprise in his eyes when he saw his trooper in the doorway. 'Jehosophat, that was quick, boy. Sure made double-quick time.'

Orlando shook his head dejectedly.

'Trouble, boss. Faldeau got sprung from custody.'

The chief jumped to his feet, his demeanour flipping to the other end of the spectrum. 'You lost him?'

'Yes, sir.'

Before the trooper could continue Brahms exploded with, 'For Christ's sake, we're a new agency. You know that. We're looking to earn our spurs in the game. And you lose a prisoner! How the hell did you manage that?'

'Got jumped by some rednecks along the trail. Didn't see it fitting for a Texan to be in a Northerner's custody was what they said.'

'Where's Faldeau now?'

Orlando shrugged. 'Dunno, boss. They just let him go. Let him have the hoss too.'

Breath came noisily from the chief's mouth. 'Ain't that a turnup for the book? I was fretting in case some pokes here in town took him and strung him up. Sure hadn't figured on nobody just taking him in order to let him go.'

'Wasn't nothing I could do about it, boss. There was three of 'em. Had me cold-decked from the start.'

The chief shook his head. 'I sure as hell tripped up. Kidding myself you got a few more brains than a rabbit. So you've just lost him and done nothing about it?'

'They took my hoss and weapon.'

'You're still walking, ain't you? Hell, must have been something you could have done.' Then he added, 'And those items come out of your salary.'

Suddenly the door opened and the mayor entered. 'Saw the trooper come back to town. Came across to see what's what,' he said as he closed the door.

'He's lost the prisoner,' the captain snorted, raising his hands in frustration. 'That's what's what!'

'How come?' the visitor asked.

Orlando repeated the story while his boss punctuated the explanation with assorted grunts of frustration.

'Bad news,' the mayor said on

completion. 'Sure don't look good for the agency.'

'Tell me something I don't know,' Brahms wheezed, shaking his head. 'I still don't understand why he didn't stay on the bastard's tail.'

'Faldeau took my hoss and weapon,' Orlando explained to the mayor. 'I thought it best I came back to report.' He looked at his boss eye to eye. 'Sir, if you'll sanction my kitting up again I'll light out after him.'

'Huh, more state equipment for you to lose?'

'I'll get him, sir,' Orlando said with determination.

'Get him? You? What can you do? You're turning out a bigger jackass than God made you in the first place.' He stomped around the cramped office, fuming, clenching and unclenching his fists, muttering expletives. He looked around his thinly populated office. 'All my other men are still tied up one way and another.'

He cursed again, then said, 'OK.

Anything to get you outa my sight. I sure don't want your greenhorn ass around here.'

He dropped back into his chair. 'Meanwhiles, I'll indent for a replacement trooper. You're only on the books till I get one.'

'Begging your pardon, sir,' Orlando said, 'that ain't fair. I just had a run of bad luck, is all.'

Brahms glowered at him and grunted.

'Hold on there, LJ,' the mayor said. 'I think the firing of Trooper Shepherd would be unwise too. State police were set up by the Federals. Wouldn't look good if you start out your operation here by firing one of their kind.'

'Huh,' the captain grunted. 'Don't look no good losing the first prisoner we clap irons on either.' He thought on it. 'OK, Orlando, get moving. But if you don't recapture the critter, don't you dare show your ass in here again.'

He studied his hands as he patted them rhythmically on the desk. 'Meanwhile, suppose I'd better wire all the agencies there's a prisoner on the loose. Boy, they're gonna love this.'

He opened the drawer and took out a photograph. A bearded Johnny Faldeau stared sullenly back at him. 'Leastways we got a picture of the renegade.'

11

Another day had passed and Johnny was making good headway. He knew enough horse lore to spell his mount regularly. And he had been lucky enough to pick up another free meal, this time with a wagon train whose trail he'd cut.

He hadn't put his mind to any long-term plans, his first objective being to get as much ground as possible between himself and the trail to the railroad and thence Austin. He was feeling easy about that. On foot, it would take the trooper some time to get back to Cardinal to report his escape; so Johnny was confident he had breathing space.

For now, the further into the wilderness of the High Plains, the better.

Holding a course by the sun he

crossed the tableland, unaware that his luck was about to change on several counts.

He was angling along a gentle bench when his horse staggered and immediately started limping. He dismounted and investigated. Treading in a gopher hole had been the cause of the trouble. He tested the horse further. No dice. Hell, wherever he was going now, he would have to walk it. Life. It dragged you down, raised you, then dropped you down again.

He breathed deep and thought about it philosophically. At least he was free and there was a healthy distance between him and the lawman. He knew the horse would hold him back and his first thought was to scoot it, letting it fend for itself. But he was in the middle of nowhere and broke. The saddle was a cashable asset; the horse had exchangeable value too: a strained ligament would mend. So he resumed his journey, painstakingly leading the injured animal.

★ ★ ★

Workers were nooning in a field. One of the children scampered over to where the adults were resting and tugged at the sleeve of an old man. He pointed south. 'The policeman, Granpappy!'

The old man squinted rheumy eyes. 'So it is. And he's returning our hoss too. He was an on-the-square boy.'

Eventually Orlando pulled in, a new badge flashing on his chest.

'Glad to see you, brother,' the old man said. 'And we got some news about where your prisoner is heading.'

★ ★ ★

Staggering across the expanse of parched grassland Johnny had watched the town gradually take shape in front of him through the hot, still air. The speck of it on the horizon had kept him going, but now the thing had become tangible, mere paces before him, he

150

began to wonder how the place could meet his needs.

He was in want of drink, food and a replacement horse. Rest too; but, against the other three requirements, rest was the only one that didn't need money. Then he told himself a town was a town, providing scope for catch-as-catch-can — he could get some bucks for the horse and rig — so he pressed on with raised hopes.

He passed the detritus that commonly marked the fringes of such settlements: abandoned wagons, garbage heaps, broken fences; then tar-paper shacks, here a tethered goat, there a scavenging dog. He paused at a corral fence to take in what was ahead and he could see respectable folk going about their business on boardwalks.

A few more yards into town and he saw the welcome label of 'Livery' on a building. He wiped grime from his face with his bandanna and knocked dust from his clothes so that he wouldn't look too much the conspicuous stranger, then presented himself. The proprietor was happy to lodge the injured animal.

'Come far?' he asked, as he took the bridle and looked at the state of the horse.

'Far enough,' Johnny said, forcing a chuckle as though it was unimportant.

The ostler looked him over, then said, 'Six bits a night. Pay me when you collect. You don't collect, I sell the rig. Horse too when he mends.'

It might fall that way, Johnny thought, but he lived in hopes. Like he'd told himself: a town provided scope for catch-as-catch-can. Aloud he said, 'Obliged' and stepped outside.

Shoving on, he soon reached the boardwalk and stepped up onto the wooden planking to drift along and intermingle with the locals.

Within seconds the smell of beef gravy hit his nostrils and his stomach groaned. Trying to ignore the aroma he continued along, passing a law office. The door of the place was open and inside he could see the weapons rack. But what really caught his eye was outside: further along on the noticeboard: a poster — with his face on it. Hell, that Yankee bastard had been quick; getting the thing printed and circulated in next to no time at all. How the hell had he got back to Cardinal so quick without a horse?

He threw the document a glance as he passed, not daring to linger, and almost collided with a chair on the boards. But he saw enough of the proclamation to figure it was a fair facsimile. There was no price posted as far as he could make out, just a few words labelling him a fugitive from justice. But that was enough trouble in itself.

His heart racing, he continued along, his hand nervously moving around his face in a vain attempt to mask his features. He crossed an alleyway to mount the next boardwalk which happened to front a hotel. Seconds later he found his way blocked by a group of men who had appeared, seemingly from nowhere, and had stationed themselves in lounging fashion on the sidewalk. He didn't cotton to having to ask his way through the throng. They wore Texas Ranger badges.

He turned on his heel to retrace his steps but now saw to his rear that the marshal had emerged from his office and was taking up residence in the chair outside, directly in front of the notice. Hell: before him the frying pan, behind him the fire.

Instinctively he right-angled into the alleyway between the marshal's office and the hotel, only to find that passage through was effectively blocked. A teamster was having trouble trying to manoeuvre a delivery wagon between the clapboards.

Johnny glanced about him. There were side steps leading up to the first storey of the hotel. He moved quickly. There was a rag lying on the back of the flatbed. He picked it up and ascended the stairs without hesitation as though that had been his intention.

At the top he began rubbing the rag over the first window he came to while he thought on the situation. The short landing went out to the front to become a narrow balcony along the façade over the main entrance, but he decided against showing himself in that direction. He moved back to another side window and found it to be raised a few inches for ventilation.

Hoping the teamster below was too occupied with his task to be paying any attention to what was going on above him, he put his fingers in the space and moved the window upwards. A quick survey showed that he was in luck, the room was vacant. He swung himself through, then pulled down the window.

The room was sparsely furnished: a double bed, dresser, wardrobe, chair. There was a pitcher and basin. Groaning in relief he took some gulps of water, then crossed to the door. He gripped the handle but let go when he heard voices in the corridor. He shot back to the window but saw that a couple of guys had joined the teamster in his task of trying to shift the wagon. Jeez, that increased the chance of his attracting attention if he tried to escape through the window.

Instead he dropped to the floor and rolled under the bed. The velour spread came down to the floor all around, effectively obscuring him. He lay there, holding his breath, trying to make sense of distant sounds. It was in that position that he fell asleep.

★ ★ ★

The first thing of which he was aware when waking was the smell of burning kerosene. He lay still, listening in the dark. Gingerly he felt the underside of the bed so close above him. There was no downward bulge nor any sound of heavy breathing. No, he was sure there was no one on the bed. He extended an arm and raised the edge of the cover overhang. There was some light in the room, a smidgeon from a low-turned oil lamp. Slowly he eased himself from under the bed and was in the act of rising when the kerosene flared into full illumination.

'What have we here?'

It was a woman's voice and he turned in its direction. The lady was sitting opposite, one hand on the lamp screw, the other holding a menacing derringer.

Johnny raised his hands. 'Sorry for the intrusion, ma'am. I don't mean no harm.'

She was maybe in her thirties, her face bone-coloured with a few delicate lines, but pretty in a refined sort of way. 'I don't think that you do,' she said. 'If you did, you wouldn't have allowed yourself to fall asleep like that. Besides, you probably realize I have no compunction about using this gun.'

He reckoned so. Any woman who, rather than screaming for help, would sit in a semi-darkened room with a stranger, was probably capable of the simple act of pulling a trigger.

'How did you know I was here?' he asked.

'I make it a practice to look under the bed each night in case there's a man there. This is the first time I've been lucky.'

'Is that a fact?' he asked in bemusement.

'No, not really, young man. Truth of the matter is your presence was obvious. Hasn't anyone told you about your snoring?'

'No.'

'Well, you're a real window-rattler. I knew I had a Rip Van Winkle as soon as I came through the door. The edges of the bed cover were flapping to and fro and the window pane sounded like it was about to shatter.' She smiled and nodded at the pitcher. 'Besides, you're a messy drinker.'

'My apologies, ma'am. Had a blue streak thirst.'

'Anyway,' she continued, 'I located the noise and cautiously investigated.

And there you were under the bed, curled up like a baby.' She smiled again. 'But if you looked like a baby, you certainly didn't sound like one.' Her eyes twinkled. 'A baby buffalo maybe.'

'I'm sorry, ma'am. It must have been quite a shock to find a stranger under your bed. Hope I didn't scare you none.'

'I got over it.'

'What happens next?'

'Depends.'

He looked hard at her. What kind of woman was this?

12

'Are you going to give me away?'

'To whom?'

'You're an intelligent woman, ma'am. I can see that. And it would be an insult to your intelligence if I was to pretend that I wasn't taking refuge here.'

'You mean — hiding from the law?'

'Yes, ma'am. But it's not like it seems. I was in a spot and I made a wrong decision.'

She left a space for him to continue, so he went on, 'Came home from the War, my pa had died, the homestead had been took over by carpet-baggers and I was broke.'

'I see. And you broke the law and now you're a wanted man.'

'Yes.'

She took further stock of him. 'What was your crime?'

He was about to answer when there came the noise of heavy feet along the corridor outside; then the distant but firm sound of knocking and somewhere a door opening.

'Get back under the bed,' she said in a low voice.

Instead he went to the window. Despite the gun still levelled at him he was taking no chances facing what sounded like a search party. He cautiously moved the drape. It was early evening so there was still some light. Below, the wagon had long since gone but there was a group of young men loafing at the corner. Looked like those damn Rangers. Hell, there was little chance of getting out through the window without him catching their attention. He decided against such an exit but by the time he had returned to the centre of the room there was a rap at the door. Nothing for it but to trust the woman. He dropped down and rolled back into place under the bed.

'Just a moment,' he heard the woman

shout; then her feet crossing the room. He quieted his breath when the door opened.

'Just checking, ma'am,' a deep voice said. 'There's news that a dangerous renegade's been seen in town.'

Jeez, he thought, things were moving fast. First the star-packing *hombre* had circulated the poster in jim-dandy time, then he was spotted within minutes in a strange town. He didn't have to put much brain time into figuring who: had to be the livery man. Shoot, that blew his chances of raising cash on the horse and rig.

'You OK, ma'am?' the deep voice continued. 'Ain't see'd nobody suspicious? A young bearded fellow.'

Johnny held his breath waiting for the disclosure but was relieved to hear her say, 'No.'

'Well, you'll let us know if you do.'

'Surely.'

'OK, ma'am. Keep your door locked.'

'Certainly, Marshal.'

The door closed. The boots clattered

on, more doors were knocked.

'You can come on out now,' he heard the woman say when the sounds had eventually faded.

Extricating himself again, he saw the derringer was once more in her hand and pointed in his direction. He followed the silent gesture of the weapon and sat on the bed.

She studied him, concluding, 'You don't look dangerous to me.'

'I wouldn't say I am, ma'am.'

She appraised him further, then nodded towards the now closed door. 'What was all that about? Have you escaped from prison?'

'Not quite, ma'am. Broke from state-police custody in transit to Austin.'

'Austin, eh? Well, you haven't told me exactly what you are wanted for.'

In his turn he'd been trying to evaluate the lady. He figured he'd got a genuine astute female in front of him and, given there was a picture of him within spitting distance giving all the particulars, he saw no point in lying. He was about to tell her the whole story when she suddenly raised her hand.

'No. Don't tell me any more. I have asked too many questions already. In answer to your question of some minutes back before we were interrupted: no, I will not give you away — as you will have gathered. At least not for the time being.' She continued her appraisal, then said, 'You look hungry.'

'I am, ma'am.'

She nodded to the jug and bowl. 'Tell you what, young man. Why don't you clean up while I order some food to be brought up?'

He hesitated. 'Have you eaten, ma'am?'

'Yes.'

'Then won't the hired help be suspicious, you ordering a second meal?'

'No. I'll say my husband has arrived.'

He looked around. 'Your husband? You're expecting your husband?'

'Yes. And I've told the manager my man is expected, so he won't see anything untoward if I say he has now arrived and requires a meal brought up to our room.' She noted his increased unease. 'But don't be alarmed. My husband is at least a stage-coach journey away.'

★ ★ ★

'I still don't know why you're doing this,' he said as he proceeded to cut another chunk out of the porterhouse steak. He was sitting at the table facing a plate overflowing with potatoes, greens and meat.

'They say not to look a gift horse in the mouth,' she said. She was sitting watching him, her gun now safely out of the way in her handbag.

'Don't get me wrong, ma'am. I'm grateful but it still don't make sense.'

'I had a son. He was younger than you but you remind me of him. Had the same penchant for getting into trouble. However, unlike you he didn't return from the War. Vicksburg.'

'Sorry to hear that, ma'am.'

'Thank you. I'm over it now, at least as much as I'll ever be.' Her eyes indicated her thoughts had gone elsewhere, then she pulled her mind back on track. 'Why did you come to this town?'

'Figured if I headed out into the High Plains I have a better chance of keeping clear of the law. Need to get myself time so that I can nail the bozo who framed me.'

'So you ended up here. Tell me, what made you pick this hotel?'

'Needed to get off the street pronto. This was the nearest place.'

She smiled. 'I'm afraid you made a mistake. You selected the worst hotel in town for your purposes. The Texas Rangers are billeted here.'

He lowered his knife and fork, his chewing activities coming to a halt. 'Huh, that explains why I saw a passel of 'em outside. Some of them are still there. What are Texas Rangers doing here? They passing through?'

'Don't think so. As I understand it they're using this hotel as a base. So, young man, you're going to have problems getting out of the building without help.'

He downed a piece of meat and looked at the darkening window. 'I can slip out when it's really dark.'

'And where will you go? Have you money, a horse?'

'No.'

'Well, now the search party has gone elsewhere and my husband is not due till tomorrow, you're in no immediate danger.' She watched him resume his eating. 'After you've finished your meal you can stay here for the night. There's spare linen in the cupboard. I think there are enough spare pillows and such to render the floor not too uncomfortable.'

He looked at her as he chewed, a puzzled look on his face. 'Can't see what your angle is, ma'am.'

'No angle. If my boy had got into trouble I'd like to think there would have been someone along the line to help him. I think I am a fair judge of character. In the short time that I've known you I've come to the conclusion that you are not inordinately evil. I may be wrong, of course. I hope not. The way I see it you're an honourable young man who has fallen on bad times. If I thought otherwise you would be back in custody, believe me. The fact is it would please me to help you. So, you'll just have to trust me. You have no option.'

'When will your husband reach here?'

'According to the stage-line schedules the earliest incoming vehicle is noon tomorrow. So you must be gone by then. And I may be able to help you in that regard too.'

'How?'

'I left Dallas quickly and just threw whatever came to hand in a case. So, fortuitously, it happens that I have some of my husband's things. You can use his shaving tackle to get rid of that beard of yours and you can have a change of clothes. That should alter your appearance enough for you to get clear. As I indicated before, when I arrived in town I familiarized myself with the stage-line's schedules. There's an outward coach at sun-up. I don't have much money, but I have enough to buy a ticket to see you on your way.'

* * *

It was early morning. He'd had a good night's sleep. So tired had he been that lying on a hard floor had not interfered with his slumber. He had shaved, decked himself out in a dark suit and taken breakfast.

The two of them were standing in the darkened doorway of the stage-line's stable watching the driver prepare the coach.

'I've been completely in your hands,

ma'am,' Johnny said. 'You could have turned me over to the law any time, but you didn't. I'm obliged for that. But I'm afraid you could be in trouble for helping me.'

She smiled. 'I don't know your name. You're a handsome young stranger whose company I have shared briefly. That is not a criminal offence.'

'A stranger to whom you have given clothing and money, asking for nothing in return. I've never met such a selfless person. A High Plains angel.'

'A poetic turn of phrase, but I'm not selfless. I've told you that you remind me of my son. That's one explanation. But, I have to admit, there is another reason behind my madness.'

'What's that? You haven't asked anything of me.'

She smiled. 'Without knowing, you have given me something.' She lowered her voice. 'I don't know your name, you don't know mine. Just as well. If you did, you might recognize it as that of a well-known business family. Now my husband and I are supposed to be socializing in Dallas. But he really only wants me there as dressing on his arm. Other than that he would prefer me not to be there. You see, he is an inveterate womanizer. We were at a function, he succumbed to the charms of some young piece of decoration and disappeared with her. He'd made an excuse about some business matter that needed urgent attention. Thought I didn't know what his game was. The upshot was, I left the function and returned to our hotel room. In the heat of the moment I threw things into a trunk — which is how I come to have some of my husband's impedimenta — and caught the first means of transport leaving Dallas. Happened to be a very early stagecoach, heading I don't know where. And here I am.'

'I don't see how I fit into all this.'

'When my dear beloved husband finds that I have gone it won't take him long to find out where the stagecoach was headed and where I alighted. I know him. He will drop everything to seek me out and he will arrive here, full of remorse. It has happened before. But this time, it will be a little different. I will not say anything but it will come to his ears that while I have been in the hotel here I have been seen in the company of another man. A handsome, young man. Taking a candlelit meal in my room, to boot.'

She smiled at the thought. 'I know him of old. He won't question me about it — he'll be too proud — but it will make him think. Hopefully remind him that I am also capable of dallying a little. Maybe this time, having a taste of what it's like will make him come to his senses. I hope so. He is a weak man in many ways but I love him in my own way and I wouldn't like our marriage to end. Now that our son is gone the big oaf is all I have left, despite his faults.'

'All aboard, sir,' the driver called.

'Well, I have to be going, ma'am,' Johnny said. He patted the coins in his pocket. 'Thanks for the money. Hope one day I can repay you.'

She chuckled. 'Don't give it another thought. I just wish it could have been more. A few dollars won't get you very far.'

'Far enough, ma'am. Anyways, obliged for all you've done. I hope things work out with your old man.'

Just before he emerged into the dawn light, she squeezed his hand. He could see moisture in her eyes. 'And I hope, young man,' she said, 'that you can clear your name and go on to lead a full life. Do it for me. God speed.'

13

'End of the line, mister,' the driver shouted down as the coach lurched to a standstill.

Johnny stepped down and looked around. 'End of the line' described it. There were the stage-line buildings — office, livery stable and corral — and little else. Half a dozen shacks and an equal number of lean-tos.

He took out his money and counted it. Less than twenty dollars. He couldn't grumble. After all, it was a handout. However, gratis or not, its paucity limited the options. Wouldn't run to a horse. A meal and bed for the night and he'd have nothing but cents in his pocket.

He looked out at the nothingness of the High Plains. Leastways, one of his problems was solved. He'd got the lawman off his back and managed not to tangle with Rangers or hick-town marshals. Furthermore he couldn't have fetched up in a more nowhere hole in the ground so, if the Yankee star-packer hadn't given up already, the critter could search till Doomsday and not find him here.

He checked the town again. An inordinate amount of noise was coming from a shack a few paces along. He moseyed over and found it unsurprisingly, labelled as a saloon. It was small but crowded and thick with smoke. Because of the amount of activity it took a long time before he could catch the attention of the barman to order a beer.

'Where do all the waddies come from?' he asked as he handed over payment. 'Town doesn't look big enough to support those kinda numbers.'

'Crew of drovers riding through on the way back from a drive. They're noisy but good for business. By the time they get down here they're a mite leaner in the purse but they still got a few dollars to jingle.'

Johnny wandered around. The men were in good humour. There were several card games in progress. Killing time in the army had seen to it that he could play a mean hand himself so, tankard in hand, he by-standered one of the games. Watching one fellow bluff a four flush to the end and get stripped, he came to the conclusion that most of them didn't know what they were doing and that a half-way decent player could win himself a hatful. That gave him an idea.

He waited till a convenient break in the play and asked his way in. He placed all his money on the table, consigned a couple of dollars to his pocket and patted the remainder. 'I'm out when that's gone if that's OK with you fellas.'

'If you play a straight game, pilgrim,' the dealer said, 'you're welcome to come and go as you please. That right, boys?'

In half an hour, with a few aces

and kickers and a sprinkling of guts, he had fifty-four dollars in front of him. He knew he could have pushed it further but when a couple of guys left creating a natural lull in the game he chose that moment to withdraw. He'd played enough games in his short life to know it wasn't healthy being greedy with strangers.

'I came in near broke, and you affable guys have provided me with a grubstake.' He took ten dollars from his pickings and dropped it on the counter, pointing to the table he had vacated. 'Drinks for my friends.'

Outside, he looked over the town again. There was a livery stable; should be able to get a horse and rig there. An eats house, where he could wrap himself round a square meal. There was no hotel, but a drovers' cottage which would serve as well. Hey, things were looking up.

★ ★ ★

The next day saw him riding out of town early. He'd purchased a horse and rig. He'd also equipped himself with a couple of canteens of water. The eats house had supplied him with beef sandwiches which he'd supplemented with jerky, hardtack and apples, not knowing when he'd next reach another settlement. He'd bought shaving tackle with the intention of keeping his features clean and as unlike the damned poster as possible. Finally, a couple of blankets had completed his kitting out.

Before leaving he'd paid a visit to the line office where there was a territory chart pinned to the wall and he'd made a mental note of the terrain.

He rode steadily across the grass flatlands, spelling his horse from time to time. During the whole day he saw no one, save for a tinker with a wagon clanking with pots and pans looking for trade in the town he had left behind him. Towards evening he kept a look-out for a likely bivouac and eventually found one: a dip sheltered by a few trees bottoming out to a small creek.

He watered his horse, set it to grazing then gathered greasewood brush for a fire. By the time night had taken a hold he'd got grub inside him and taken a smoke. Bushed with a day's riding, he wrapped a blanket around him and fell fast asleep while the fire shoved back the night shadows.

★ ★ ★

'I'd recognize that suit of clothes anywheres!'

The voice that jerked Johnny into wakefulness was hard. His body rigid with adrenalin he turned to find himself looking into the black-hole end of a Colt. The man behind it wore similar garb. Johnny didn't have to ask who it was.

'Messing around with my missus,' the man went on, clicking back the hammer, 'that ranks with hoss-stealing in my book. And merits the same punishment. Range justice I think they call it out here.'

His face was shaped like a pear, point downwards, with a moustache in the middle of it. The beetroot skin was puffy and blue-veined. So this was the good woman's spouse. God knows why she wanted to hang on to such a specimen. But the solution of that conundrum had low priority on Johnny's mind at that moment. 'You got me wrong, mister. Ain't messed around with nobody's missus.'

The man shook his head. 'Don't give me that crud. You're the jasper all right.' Behind him dawn was already spreading its glow across the sky. 'Got your description from the guy in the hotel, so I know you're the one.' He nodded to the jacket that Johnny had draped over the saddle beside him. 'Then there's my suit you're been creasing and covering in trail crap. I ain't used to this trailing game but I was in luck. Came across a tinker, told him you and I were pardners and he pointed me in the right direction.' The rheumy eyes were glazed with unredemptive determination. 'Nobody messes with my missus and gets away with it.'

'I told you, mister. I didn't mess with her.'

'You spent the night in her room,' Pear-Face went on.

'Yeah, but I was hiding out is all,' Johnny countered. 'The place was crawling with Rangers. Couldn't budge. Last thing on my mind was dishonouring a lady. Get it straight. And she had nothing to do with me holing up in her room. I forced her to hide me out till it was clear to make a get-away.'

The man grunted dismissively. 'My woman begged me on her knees not to come a-chasing you. That confirms that you and her were up to no good.'

'No it don't. Listen, mister, I ain't done nothing to justify you blowing my head off.'

The man ignored him and straightened his arm, eyeing the young man along the barrel in preparation. Johnny gritted his teeth. He'd felt death coming many times while he was in uniform. Looking along the wrong end of that gun barrel in the middle of nowhere brought back the familiar feeling. There were two options: leap for the man, or roll away.

Going for the man seemed the most foolhardy, so he steeled himself in preparation to heave himself sideways. Maybe he could get enough impetus into rolling down the grade to make himself a more awkward target. Wouldn't do much good, he figured. He hadn't got a weapon to make a grab for and the guy was only yards away. There was no cover to speak of, so if the guy missed first time and was the worst shot this side of the Pecos he was sure to be on target with at least one of the other five live ones in the chamber.

'Don't pull that trigger or you're a dead man.'

Both equally startled, Johnny and his ambusher looked in the direction of the voiced intrusion.

'Relax your grip on the weapon and drop it,' the voice continued.

The order was backed up by an ugly-looking Remington which, in turn, was held menacingly by a dust-covered wraith who had appeared from nowhere and was now standing, legs apart, on the brim of the ridge.

Johnny was as stunned as Pear-Face but his surprise didn't prevent him from taking advantage of the fact that in the investigatory movement the man's Colt had veered away from him. He rolled out of danger to come to his feet, grinning in a mixture of incredulity and relief.

'Now drop it,' Orlando said, continuing to address the aggrieved husband. 'You won't be hurt 'less you make the wrong move.'

'What's a Yank doing prodding into this?' Pear-Face snarled.

'This Yank is a State Trooper,'

Orlando informed him. 'And we Yanks get very impatient at times. Like now.'

Pear-Face's jaw dropped. Eventually he came back with, 'Well, if you're a lawman, you got no reason to shoot me.'

'Every reason,' Orlando went on. 'That man is my prisoner and you are interfering with a lawman in pursuance of his duty. You put a hole in him, and I put a hole in you.'

'I don't believe this,' Pear-Face grunted, still trying to get his brain round the situation.

'I don't care what you believe, mister,' Orlando said giving emphasis by a slight but ominous wave of the Remington's barrel, 'as long as you drop the gun.'

The man complied and the trooper light-footed down the grade to pick up the fallen weapon. He shucked out the loads and threw it at the man. 'I heard about your doings in town,' he said. 'Whatever you think this man has done wrong is nothing compared with the official charge against him: murder. That takes precedence in the justice book. I've seen your horse tethered back a-ways. Now get on it and head back to town.'

The man backed away. 'I'll go back all right. And I'll tell the authorities about your actions. I'm a tax-paying citizen with a justifiable grievance.'

'That's the idea. I want you to do just that. The Texas Rangers back there know of my operation. Tell them State Trooper Orlando Shepherd has retaken custody of Johnny Faldeau and is resuming his mission in escorting the prisoner to Austin. And tell them to wire the information to the office in Cardinal.'

The man didn't move.

'Have you got that, Mr Grieving Taxpayer?'

The man grunted an affirmation and walked up the grade, pausing at the top to look back.

Orlando caught the scowl he was throwing at him. 'And if you cause me any trouble,' he shouted, 'I'll take you in as well.'

'And look after that missus of yours better too,' Johnny shouted. 'You got a fine woman there if only you knew it.'

The man looked at the two of them for a moment and then began to walk away.

'Stay here,' Orlando said to Johnny and mounted the incline to monitor the fellow's actions. When he was at last satisfied the man was on his way he returned to Johnny's makeshift camp-site.

'Never thought I'd be glad to see you again, Yank,' Johnny said as the trooper rejoined him. 'That bozo was ready to ventilate me for sure. I owe you one.'

'Oh, no you don't. Don't freight the idea I was saving your hide. Like I told him, I was retaking custody of my prisoner is all.'

Johnny shook his head. 'Ought to have let him finish the job,' he said in a mock philosophical tone. 'Would have saved you a job and the state the expense of a hanging.'

'You don't get it, do you, Reb? Ain't my concern what happens to you once I've delivered you. You're my responsibility up to and till that point. Ain't nobody gonna stand in my way of achieving that. That simple objective is all I'm bothered about. Now get yourself ready to move out.'

Johnny walked over to his saddle and picked up the jacket. 'Well, sure glad you showed up,' he said as he pulled on the garment. Then he chuckled. 'Hell, I never figured I'd have a Yank on my ass who could hold a trail as good as some ground-nosing Dixie hound.'

14

With a sack of flour and a bag of coffee beans stacked in front of him Anxiety Jones staggered out of the dry goods store on Logan's main street. Guilt about Johnny's situation had been bearing down on his shoulders and he had decided to get out. The youngster was a good kid and deserved a helping hand. Anxiety knew he was the only one who could help. The way he figured it, once he had made the break with the gang and got Veener clear, then he could tell the law everything he knew, and how he was sure Wallace had fingered Johnny.

Moving along the boardwalk with his burden he suddenly came face to face with Wallace.

'Howdy, Anxiety. Some bundle you're toting there. You stocking up for the season?'

'Hi, there, Hal. Er, no, just regular supplies.' That was not true. Anxiety aimed to get Veener to safety and to put as much ground as he could between them and Logan before he began doing any talking. That meant travel; and travel meant provisioning.

'You're not going anywheres, are you, Anxiety?'

'Hell, no, sir.'

'Then you got time for a drink.'

'Sure thing, Mr Wallace.'

'Well, haul them bags into the Forty-Five.'

As they entered the saloon Wallace ordered a bottle and glasses, giving an unseen signal for strong liquor. The bartender winked and brought them over to the table. Wallace indicated for him to fill the glasses, then raised his drink in salutation. After Anxiety had drained his glass, Wallace refilled it for him. As the oldster downed it, Wallace watched him saying, 'You are aiming to light a shuck, Anxiety.'

He replenished the oldster's glass. 'I

hear tell you bought a wagon and hid it behind that adobe of yours. And you been quietly provisioning it.'

Anxiety was cold-decked. 'OK, it's been on my mind about moving on. I was leaving it till the last minute to say *adios*, is all.' He downed the drink nervously. 'I'm pulling up my picket pin, Hal. It's for the best.'

Wallace filled the old man's glass yet again. 'After all our time together? Hell, Anxiety, you're my number one.'

'Sorry, Hal, there comes a time to move on. That's the way of the West.'

'Hey, you and I have been together a spell. There's more to it than just moving on.'

Anxiety looked at his boss for a time, slung back the drink in search of courage, then said, 'You and I know Johnny didn't kill that bank fellow in Cardinal. You wanted Johnny out of the way so you did for the old man and tried to pin it on the kid. I didn't have to be there to know that.' He hadn't intended to expose such thoughts but the deliberately plied drink had dulled his common sense.

'You got it wrong, Anxiety.'

The old man's lips formed a skew-whiffed smile. 'They say never kid a kidder.'

Wallace shrugged in apparent capitulation.

'Fact is,' Anxiety went on, 'that bank haul gave me all I need. I ain't got many years left and there's enough in my saddle-bags now to help my girl and see me through my last days. Figure I'll ride south. Find myself a little place near the border to smoke my pipe and watch the clouds pass by.'

Wallace nodded. 'Can't argue with that. That's what the green stuff's for at the end of the day.'

'You been good to me, Hal. So there's no way I'd put the finger on you. Not that I could. I ain't got anything that would stand up in court. But the kid knows you did it. And he knows he won't get anything out of you or the boys to clear his name, so he'll come looking for me. I'm his last resort and I figure he'll try to hound something out of me. That puts me in a cleft stick. I like Johnny. I remember him when he was in knee britches. Liked his old man too. But I can't help the boy, and yet I don't want to disappoint him. So the best thing is to make myself scarce.'

'I can't persuade you to stay on?'

'Nope. I've thought it out, made up my mind. This is where our trails part.'

Wallace picked up the bottle and was about to pour another into Anxiety's glass but the old man stopped him. 'No more, thanks. One thing I've learned in life, it's best to keep goodbyes short.' He bent down and picked up his bags. 'Thanks for putting some change in an old man's pockets. Say *adios* to the boys for me.'

Wallace smiled, nodded and watched him go to the door. 'Keep your powder dry, old-timer.'

The batwings flapped on his departure and Wallace took his glass and bottle to the bar. As he was sipping contemplatively a man with a pigtail rolled in.

'Ahoy there,' Wallace said, nodding to the back room. 'I got a job for you, Lenny.'

★ ★ ★

Their horses had put in a good morning's legwork when Orlando suddenly reined in. 'What's that yonder?' he said, pointing away to their flank across the sward. 'Looks like a wagon.'

Johnny brought his own horse to standstill and squinted. 'It is too.'

Orlando shielded his eyes. 'Somebody in trouble I figure. Wagon's at a mighty strange angle.' He looked ahead. 'By my reckoning we should be cutting the railroad soon.' He looked back at the wagon, pondered on it then said, 'Guess we should ride over and check it out.'

'Anything you say, boss.'

The trooper wheeled his horse. 'And behave yourself.'

As they neared they could see a woman in levis labouring at the side of the awkwardly-tilted wagon. It had lost a back wheel.

'State Police,' Orlando declared as they pulled in. 'Looks like you could do with another pair of hands there, miss.'

'Oh, thank God,' she said, straightening from her task and using the back of her hand to move away the hair that was cascading over her eyes.

The trooper touched his hat to an old woman sitting on a rock. 'Ma'am,' he said, then turned back to the girl. 'Where you headed, miss?'

'We were heading west but things didn't work out. My father suddenly had some kind of spasm and died quickly afterwards. Heart attack, Ma reckons. So we've buried him and are now trying to get back. Town called Acacia is the next place, if I remember.'

Orlando cast his mind back and recalled a faded name on a board. 'That's right. Couple of hours back aways. We came through the place. Well, missy, let's see what we can do here.'

He dismounted and indicated for Johnny to do likewise. The trooper tethered the animals some distance away, then undid the cuffs. 'Stand over there,' he said in a low voice, pointing to the far side, 'and keep away from the horses. We might be acting the good Samaritans here but, remember, I'll still be watching you.'

'You got the burr?' he asked the girl.

'Yes,' she said, pointing to the wheel-nut lying on the box seat. 'Found it some yards back.'

Orlando cast an eye over the horizontal wheel, felt the spokes. 'Wheel's still in good shape. Get under the wagon, Johnny, and see if there's any damage to the frame.'

Johnny eased himself beneath the

vehicle and made an inspection. 'Can't see any cracks in the structure,' he said as he re-emerged into the sunlight. The stiffness in his leg was apparent as he got to his feet.

'Then it's just a simple matter of getting the wheel back in place,' the other said. 'I'll see if I can support it. You got that crook leg, ain't you?' He put his back to the wagon, bent his knees and tested the weight. 'Yeah, should be able to do it.' He walked round the back, took stock of the contents. 'But we're gonna have to get all the heavy stuff out, miss. Don't like the look of that stove for a start.'

After a while the stove along with boxes, jars, small barrels, and varied kitchen paraphernalia were laid out on the ground.

Orlando stepped away and took off his shirt. 'I noted you got some butter amongst your gear, miss. Put a heap on the axle. Needs greasing.' He waited until she had done so, then gestured for his companion to take charge of the wheel as he himself approached the side of the vehicle. He paused until Johnny had the wheel righted and to hand, then placed his back against the wagon. He bent his legs, gripped the underside and took a deep breath.

Muscles taut, young body bunched, he took the strain. Then, closing his eyes, he heaved and the wagon creaked upwards. With a little adjustment this way and that, the hub was soon firmly in place on the axle. Orlando waited till his breathing was back to normal, then fixed the nut and stood back to admire the result. 'There you are, miss. Stick to flat trail and you'll be safely in Acacia in no time.'

'I don't know how to thank you,' the girl said.

'Well, if I can have something for a wipe down,' Orlando said indicating his sweaty torso.

'Of course.' She found a towel and handed it to him, adding, 'And if we can get a fire going I'll make some coffee.'

'Sure could do with a cup, miss,' Orlando said. He looked around and saw abundant tinder. 'I'll start the fire while Johnny reloads your wagon for you.'

'Yessa, boss,' the other said in a mock Jim Crow voice and moved over to the contents. He considered the exercise and asked, 'Like to tell me how you want it stacking, miss?'

The girl joined him to supervise the reloading and, for the first time the old lady stirred. While the other three set about their tasks she rooted about in one of the boxes and extracted a blackened coffee pot.

Once the fire was crackling healthily, Orlando wiped himself again with the towel and prepared to pull on his shirt. He didn't see Johnny pause in his loading chores and stand watching him. The Texan was shifting the pots and pans at the time and at that moment had an iron skillet in his hand.

The trooper's head disappeared into his shirt and all he knew was, when his head re-emerged again, it received an almighty whap. He dropped heavily like a corrida bull.

Johnny looked down at the crumpled form. 'Real sorry about that, pal.'

He glanced at the females and saw they had both been shaken rigid by his action. 'Don't worry about him, ladies. I ain't killed him. Just hit him hard enough to sleep for a spell.'

The young girl ran over and knelt beside the trooper as Johnny relieved him of his gun and threw it far into the grass.

'What did you do this for?' she asked, after she had checked the fallen man was still breathing.

'Ain't got time to talk, miss,' he said. 'It's just that me and him are going different ways is all.'

He moved quickly over to the front of the wagon where he had seen a Winchester. 'I'll take this and drop it a few yards yonder,' he said, as he picked it up. 'Can't leave you out here on the plains without a weapon but I don't want you trying anything foolish.'

He returned to where the girl was kneeling beside the trooper's still form and looked down. 'The bozo's got quite a lump coming up there,' he said. 'Put some of that fancy butter of yours on it and he'll be as right as rain in no time.' He chuckled. 'Save for a headache and cutting a shindy at being parted from his pardner.'

He strode to the horses. 'I'm taking his horse too. Don't want him complicating things by haring after me again.'

Untethering the animals, he mounted up and gave the ladies one last look. 'You wanted to know how you could thank him. Well, give him another cup of that coffee and take him on to Acacia with you. He'll appreciate that.'

He grinned and gigged his horse. A hundred yards on he slowed and raised the Winchester high so they could see it. He lowered it to the grass then dug in his heels once more.

★ ★ ★

Atop a swaleback ridge he reined in. Ahead stretched more of the High Plains, right to the horizon: a lost piece of nowhere, ideal for a guy to get lost in.

He dismounted to spell his horse and took stock of the situation. Hiding out in the middle of nowhere. But what then? At some time or other he needed to get to Logan. He couldn't postpone it for ever. Then his thoughts moved to another course of action. Why not now?

The trooper didn't know he would be heading there. And anyway the Northerner had his own troubles with no horse. Moreover, it didn't matter too much if his poster had reached the town's law office. Without his beard he had a new face. And he was dressed differently too. Looked more like a drummer than a fugitive. Surely, he could remain unrecognized long enough to do what he had to.

By the time he figured that his horse had rested enough he had made up his mind. Logan, next stop. Then Wallace.

★ ★ ★

Orlando sat recuperating in the shade of the wagon. The girl had bathed his head and he had got sustenance from several cups of coffee. There was no way he was going to report back to his redneck boss that he'd lost the prisoner yet again. But what should be his next step? The girl had told him which direction Faldeau had ridden off but he didn't know the fellow's ultimate destination; and he himself had no horse for pursuit anyhow.

Then it dawned on him. A long shot. He did have a name. Logan, the name on the army paper in Faldeau's sweatband. The young man had dismissed it as unimportant: a home town to which he hadn't returned. But he could have been bluffing. And it was the only clue Orlando had. Better than nothing.

He rose and walked to the front of the wagon. There were two horses.

'I need one of your horses, miss,' he said. It would mean riding bareback but he had done that before as a youngster. Horse racing had been a pastime amongst the workers back home and they couldn't afford the luxury of saddles.

'One horse should be able to cope with pulling your wagon,' he said.

'You sure?' the girl asked hesitantly.

'It'll be a strain for him but Acacia is not far. If you stick to the trail and take it slow he should do it.'

15

Johnny crested the ridge that marked the shallow run in to Logan. He paused long enough to satisfy himself he recognized the town below, then plunged downwards. He cut off from the trail and swung up through a break in the timber. Soon he was approaching Anxiety's cabin. There were no horses outside so if the old-timer was in he would be alone with Veener. He drew rein, dismounted and knocked on the door.

It was Veener who opened it.

'Johnny,' she said, surprise in her voice. 'I thought . . . '

He smiled. 'I'll tell you about it. Where's your pa?' he said, taking off his hat and accepting her gestured invitation to enter.

'Oh, Johnny, Johnny,' she said when back inside; and she dropped heavily into a chair.

'What's the matter?' he asked.

'Pa's dead. Buried him yesterday.'

It was Johnny's turn to drop into a chair. 'Jesus, I'm sorry, Veener. How? When?'

She started crying and he crossed over to pacify her. After some sniffing she pulled herself together. 'Seems there had been a shooting. They found him in an alleyway with another fellow. Both shot dead.'

'Who was the other guy?'

'Had the look of a sailor.'

'Name of Lenny?'

'Yes, that was it.'

While he was letting the information sink in she added, 'Just before we were leaving too.'

'Leaving?'

'Yes. Ever since you disappeared Pa was agitated. Couldn't rest. I knew something was wrong but didn't know what and he wouldn't tell me. Then suddenly he said we were leaving. Just like that. I think he felt guilty about something. Once I caught him muttering to himself; he seemed to be saying he was going to do the right thing by you. I didn't understand and when I asked him he went quiet. Do you know what it was all about?'

'I got an idea.' He paused then asked, 'Did Wallace know about his plans?'

'I don't know.'

He thought on it. 'Did your pa buy any extra supplies?'

'Yes. And a wagon. It's out back.'

'Then there's every chance Wallace would have knowed.' So Wallace had got Lenny to kill the old man. Either Anxiety had put up some resistance and managed to take Lenny with him — or Wallace had wiped out Lenny for some reason, like he'd tried to do with Johnny. Either way, Wallace was behind it.

'Do you know about Wallace and your pa's involvement with him?' he asked.

'Just that he helped Mr Wallace with some jobs from time to time.'

'And that's all?'

She nodded. 'Yes. He'd always lived by doing odd jobs for folk for as long as I could remember. Used to help your pa out, didn't he?'

Johnny nodded. So the old-timer hadn't told his daughter about his criminal life. Seemed reasonable. He would have been the same if he had had anyone close. One thing Johnny knew: it wasn't up to him to put a cloud over a father's memory and he remained silent.

'You must have travelled far,' she said, breaking the lull as she regained composure. 'You could do with refreshment. I'll make coffee.'

'That'd be fine.'

While she was absent in the kitchen he thought things over. Wallace had done to Anxiety what he had tried to do to Johnny. Wallace had learned the old man wanted out and he had paid the price for it. Furthermore the bit about 'doing right by Johnny' had all the markings of Anxiety wanting to clear Johnny with the law about the bank killing. Well, now Anxiety was gone the situation had changed. There was nothing stopping him from at last putting the finger on Wallace. Plus he had another reason, just as strong, for making Wallace pay his dues. The more he thought about the old man's fate, the more resolved he became.

Snag was, he hadn't got a gun. He cursed himself that it hadn't been long since he'd had the state trooper's pistol in his hand; but he'd left it for the man to find.

He joined Veener in the kitchen. 'Would you think it brassy if I asked to have your pa's gun and belt. You know, as a memento?'

'That's an odd memento,' she said, without looking up from her task.

'I know, but I never got around to kitting myself out. And a guy needs an iron out here.'

'Certainly. I have no use for them. You'll find them in the top drawer in the cupboard in his room.'

Johnny found the weapon, an old Dragoon. There were enough shells on the belt for a full chamber or two and he sat on the chair in the parlour while he loaded it. He swung the belt around his hips, buckled it, then tried a few draws.

'I was surprised when you left without saying goodbye,' she said from the kitchen.

'Me too,' he replied.

'What was that about?'

'I'll get round to telling you,' he said, hefting the weapon to get the feel of it.

'All very mysterious.'

'Yeah. That's what I thought,' he said absently while he made a final check over the gun.

He holstered it and returned to the kitchen. 'Listen, Veener,' he said apologetically, 'do you mind if I backtrack on the coffee? I've just remembered I've got some pretty urgent business in town. The news about your pa blew it straight out of my mind.'

'Of course not. It'll keep.'

★ ★ ★

He made the town and hitched his horse at the end, a long ways away from the Forty-Five. He strolled along the boardwalk, mulling over how he was going to handle this. He suddenly realized he was acting hot-headed and needed to calm down, to think things out rationally.

He stopped when he got in clear sight of the saloon and rested against a storefront. He stayed that way for a while, watching the comings and goings. He still hadn't quite worked out a plan when his brain was jerked into the hard present.

'I figured you'd be coming back here.'

Johnny recognized the voice before he turned to see the familiar Yankee face. 'How the hell did you know?' he demanded of the trooper. 'And how did you get here so quick?'

Orlando moved from the alleyway up on to the boardwalk and joined the fugitive. 'Ways and means.'

Johnny was now away from the wall against which he had been leaning and was facing the lawman. 'How'd you reckon I'd be heading for Logan?'

'You were claiming you'd been framed. Figure you'd take it upon yourself to try to do something about it. You told me you hadn't been back here, but Logan was the only name I had. It was a long shot, but it's paid off.'

Johnny backed away and his hand fell close to the butt of Anxiety's Dragoon. 'Not quite, Trooper. You haven't got me yet. I don't want to use this — but if you force me . . . '

'Don't be stupid,' Orlando said in a matter-of-fact tone. 'Relax that gunhand, give me the weapon and let's talk.'

'What have we got to jaw about? You

just want to get those damn cuffs on me again.'

The trooper shrugged. 'Ain't denying that. It's my job. But not immediately. Now we've come this far we might as well exchange a few words and see what we can clear up. Come on, Johnny, give me your gun.'

For a moment Johnny regarded the other man sullenly, with only half-concealed resentment, then resignedly pulled the gun and handed it to him butt first. 'What do you mean — we?'

Orlando pushed the gun into his belt and looked across the street at the Forty-Five. 'We need somewhere to talk. We're a mite open to view here. What about over there?'

'That's the last place,' Johnny said knowingly and turned to head back down the street. 'There's another gin palace along the block.'

He pushed through the batwings and advanced to the bar. 'Couple of shots of sour mash.'

The barkeep complied and a minute

later the two were seated with their drinks away from the ears of other patrons.

'Give me some names,' Orlando began, 'and tell me what you were aiming to do.'

'Fellow who runs the Forty-Five, name's Wallace. Uses the place as a cover for rustling and bank robbing.'

'The bank job back in Cardinal job — was that his?'

'Yes. And a lot more before I came on the scene.'

Orlando nodded. 'We know a gang's been operating locally. This could be it.'

'Well, Wallace is the big honcho. Got a couple of playmates, two hardcases, name of Mort and Dave. There was another member of the bunch, an old pal of mine by the name of Anxiety Jones. But I've just learned he got bellied-up when he tried to cut out from the gang.'

'How did you learn that?'

'Lived with his daughter in an adobe

just out of town. I just came from there. Good news is, seems the old man took one of the hardcases with him. So, including Wallace, they're down to three now.'

'This Anxiety Jones, he the reason why you wouldn't put the finger on the Wallace bunch before?'

'Yeah. But nothing stopping me now.'

'And you were one of the gang?'

'For a short spell. Have to admit that. I'd just got back from army hospital. Found my old man had died and the family farm had been lost. I had no jack and little prospect of employment on account of the crook leg. Wallace ran this shady operation, stealing from carpetbaggers and it had appeal. But I soon found out they were a trigger-happy bunch. They killed a guy during a rustling caper and I wanted out. Wallace put pressure on me to do one last job with him: the Cardinal bank. But he didn't cotton to the notion of me going my own way and, as I figure it, he killed the bank man and pinned it on me. Must have aimed to kill me too but things went wrong for him at the last minute and he couldn't pull it off. A lucky chain of circumstances: I didn't carry a gun, the bank man's derringer was unloaded and his own gun was jammed, so he couldn't put a slug through my head.'

'Is there any hard evidence he killed the bank man?'

'None. I figure Anxiety knew and was gonna tell the law but he's history now.'

'So how was you gonna sort out the mess yourself?'

'Face Wallace, I reckon I could make him talk.'

The trooper permitted himself a restrained smile. 'And you think you'd have pulled that off?'

Johnny remained silent.

'Seems to me you're being a mite hot-headed here,' the trooper went on. 'Ain't thought things out at all.'

Johnny pondered on it, then came

up with, 'Now you're here I could challenge him in your presence. You'd be a witness to whatever I could get out of him.'

'He's not going to confess just like that.'

'Give me a few minutes with him; I'll get something out of him.'

'Statements made under duress ain't worth nothing.' The trooper mulled things over. 'Are you on the level about these bozos?'

'As square as about anything I've been in my life.'

The trooper studied his eyes for a time. 'Figure you are. Tell you what I'll do. It'll mean I'm putting my job on the line, that is if I've still got one. When I first hit town I made myself known to the local marshal. Feller named Wilson, Sid Wilson. I couldn't tell him much because there was little I knew and I was only playing a hunch. Anyway, he offered his co-operation. Now I've got some idea what it's all about, I can put him in the picture. Then we'll take the Wallace crew into custody on suspicion of the crimes you've listed. But you've got to play this straight. That means you do everything I say. And, of course when it's all over, I have to put the cuffs on you too; you gotta realize that. But if you've been telling me the truth about all this, things shouldn't go too bad for you.'

Finishing his drink, Johnny shrugged. 'Ain't got nothing to lose. Let's see this Marshal Wilson and get things moving.' He stood up.

Orlando rose too but hesitated to take the lead.

'You can go in front,' Johnny said with a smile. 'I promise I won't bop you on the head again.'

When they turned up at the law office they found Marshal Wilson cleaning his gun. Orlando introduced Johnny and between the two of them they explained the situation.

'All this is fitting into place,' Wilson observed at the conclusion of the story.

He pointed to documents on his desk. 'Got a pile of papers from head office about a spate of crimes all round the county. Never figured it was being masterminded under my very nose. So it's Wallace, eh?' He shook his head. 'Would never have believed it. He's a smart one, using the Forty-Five as a cover. But it all fits.'

'We can take them into custody now,' Orlando said. 'Faldeau is willing to turn State's Evidence.'

The marshal nodded as he absorbed the idea.

'You got a deputy?' the trooper went on. 'We could use some back-up on this.'

The marshal shook his head. 'This is only a hick town. Funds don't run to such luxuries.' Then he gestured towards Johnny. 'Like I said I'll co-operate with a fellow law officer but I'm not happy about Faldeau's involvement. I know he's got an interest in how this turns out but I'd feel better about the matter if he was behind bars where he belongs. This is a formal law operation now.'

Johnny stiffened but Orlando raised a placating hand. 'He's a material witness, Marshal, and I trust him. You've got my word he'll be OK. Besides, if you haven't got a deputy we'll need him. There are three hardcases out there who won't cotton to the idea of being took.'

The marshal shrugged in reluctant acceptance. 'Have it your way. But he's your responsibility.'

'We'll stow them in your jail for the time being,' Orlando continued, 'but the case is bigger than the county. The prisoners will have to be transported to Austin. We'll keep them here and I'll telegraph headquarters. Figure the state police will call in the federals. They've got the staff and equipment for shipping prisoners long distances.'

'Anything you say, Trooper,' Wilson said. 'I'm just a local man. You know more about these things than I do.' He slipped his newly cleaned gun into its

219

holster and stood up. 'But I do know my town, so this is the way we'll play it. First, we've got to size up the lay of the land. No point in sashaying into the Forty-Five at half-cock. We don't know what we're walking into. You stay here for a spell while I take a mosey over there and check who's about. Better me than you. Nobody'll think anything suspicious, me doing my regular round.'

Orlando nodded.

16

It was some ten minutes later that the marshal returned. 'We're in luck,' he said. 'The three of them are in the back room. Couldn't be better.'

'How do you get to this back room?' the trooper asked.

'Through the saloon,' the marshal explained. 'It's the door next to the stairs.'

Johnny nodded. 'I know it.'

'You got three sets of handcuffs?' Orlando asked.

The marshal crossed to a cupboard. 'Somewhere.' Eventually he located the items, blew the dust off them and held them up for inspection.

'OK,' the trooper said. 'One final thing. Open the cell door in readiness so we can walk them straight in.'

* * *

Wilson led the way into the Forty-Five. Business was quiet, just a couple of girls and a handful of men at various tables. The marshal passed close to where the largest group was playing monte. He stopped with his back to a silent piano. Standing conspicuously in the centre of the room, he covered the place with a stony stare that lasted long enough to get everyone's attention. 'Law business, boys,' he said in a voice, low but authoritative. He jerked his thumb at the doorway. 'Out, now. All of you. The girls included. And make it quiet.'

Stopped in their activities, the folk saw he meant business and complied with puzzled expressions on their faces.

Wilson looked at the bartender, his face bathed in the light coming from the oil-lamp that hung above the bar. 'They still in there?'

'Yes, sir.'

'OK. You make yourself scarce too.'

With another 'Yes, sir' the man put down the glass he was wiping and disappeared through the door behind the bar.

In the now empty saloon Wilson pulled out his gun and raised it in silent indication for his companions to do likewise. Slowly he walked to the door of the back room. He paused, then turned the knob, flinging wide the door.

'Nobody move,' he said, striding smartly inside. He moved crab-wise so that he remained in sight of his companions and gestured for them to enter.

With Orlando in the vanguard, the pair proceeded towards the doorway.

Before they had time to see the room was empty there came the creak of feet on boards behind them and a voice boomed out, 'Hold it right there!'

They turned. Wallace and his two hardcases had entered through the door used for exit by the barman and were now standing behind the bar, guns levelled. Realization moved across the trooper's face. They had been duped by Wilson. The man was in Wallace's pay and had used his earlier scouting out the situation as a pretext to warn the crooked saloon owner.

'Get out of the line of fire, Sid,' Wallace said to the lawman. 'You've done your bit.'

The delay was enough for Johnny. The lines of surprise that had suddenly webbed his features disappeared and he leapt back into the saloon, upending a table for cover. Guns discharged and splinters chunked out of the table. Johnny pulled the Dragoon and returned fire.

At the same time Orlando nipped behind the door jamb, spinning round to see Wilson raising his gun behind him. The trooper's weapon roared and the lawman's legs buckled.

Back in the main parlour the gunfire had rolled into one continuing explosion. Johnny took measure of the situation. He knew the disintegrating table was no permanent cover. There was only one piece of furniture in the place within reach and solid enough to provide some safety — the piano. And he had one advantage: unlike anyone else in the deafening exchange he was used to being under fire and it didn't faze him. He steeled himself, then leapt forward in a crouch, staging a weaving trajectory between the tables, firing as he went.

However, over the final stretch his weak leg crumpled, painfully bringing him to the boards. But he turned his collapse into a roll so that he fetched up behind the instrument which began clanging out a discordant concerto when bullets cut through the wood and into the strings.

The gang's advantage was that they had the bar as cover — but they still had to show themselves above it to fire. Orlando's gun barked from the backroom and caught the exposed Mort in the neck. The white-haired man stumbled, coughed and pitched clear of cover, his gun falling from nerveless fingers.

Now it was two against two.

Snag was Orlando and Johnny only had one gun apiece and those were nearly empty while the Wallace crew, on home territory and prepared, probably had an armoury behind the bar. Then Johnny noticed the oil-lamp suspended from the ceiling above the bar. Keeping to the floor he showed himself from the other side of the piano, just long enough to take a pot at the lantern above the cropped head of Dave, Wallace's remaining sidekick. It was a quick action and the Texan had to withdraw to cover so he didn't see the effect.

But he heard it. The lamp exploded showering the back of the bar with burning liquid. There was a scream, then Wallace, his clothes flicked with flames, sprang out shooting blind and wild, making for the door. Johnny took a fast bead on him but his hammer clicked on an empty chamber.

Orlando advanced cautiously from the back room. There were screams coming from behind the bar and he could see the reflection of flames in the glasses and the polished wood above it. He progressed further, stepping over the body of Mort, and looked behind the bar. Dave was a human torch, rolling on the floor.

Meanwhile, intent now only on nailing Wallace, Johnny dashed to the front doorway and paused in the cover of the batwings to reload. Then he edged out onto the boardwalk.

Behind him Orlando had grabbed bar towels and was vainly trying to put out the flames that engulfed the screaming Dave.

Outside Johnny could make out the far figure of Wallace making for horses at a hitchrail. In his war days Johnny was used to firing over distance. He raised his gun, slowly took aim and fired. Wallace keeled over, caught in the leg. But it must have been a superficial wound because it wasn't sufficient to keep him down. He limped to his feet and turned to face his adversary.

His crook leg paining, Johnny advanced, gun still levelled. 'The game's over, Hal,' he said. 'That guy with me is a state trooper. He knows everything about your operation.'

Folks watched from windows and doorways as Johnny limped along the street but he was unaware of them. All he knew now was that he was close enough to kill Wallace. But he wanted him alive. With Anxiety and Mort dead, and Dave probably gone the same way, Wallace was the only man who could clear him.

He stopped with yards between them, so that muzzle faced muzzle. 'You're gonna tell the trooper how you framed me for the banker's killing if it's the last thing you do,' he said.

'The hell I will,' Wallace snarled and pulled the trigger.

Feeling something hot score his ribs, Johnny dived to one side, instinctively returning fire.

From his downed position he saw the worn soles of Wallace's unmoving boots. He dragged himself to his feet wincing at the pain in his side and limped over to the fallen man. Wallace's expensive shirt was staining fast on the chest.

Aware of Orlando now beside him, Johnny knelt down and grabbed Wallace by the collar. 'Tell the trooper the truth, Hal. You got nothing to lose now.'

'Ain't that a turn up for the book?' Wallace croaked. 'A Yank with a star! And you a Reb!'

'Tell him for God's sake,' Johnny persisted.

'I'll tell him. Don't listen to his whining, Lawman. Faldeau was a crook just like the rest of us. That bank job in Cardinal — he panicked at the last minute. Shot the bank manager. Write that down in your book, Lawman.'

'That ain't the truth, and you know it,' Johnny snarled. 'Clear your conscience for God's sake.'

'See you in hell, soldier boy,' Wallace wheezed and went limp.

Johnny continued shaking the slack figure. 'Tell him, damn you, tell him!'

Wallace's eyes remained open, their harsh stare slipping into vacancy.

'It's no use, Johnny,' Orlando said. 'He's dead.'

Johnny let out a long breath of his own while he looked at the blanching face. 'What about the others?'

'All dead.'

'Don't know if any of them would have cleared me anyhow.'

He stood up, wincing and feeling his side. 'Well, reckon this is the end of the line.'

'You've been hit,' Orlando observed. 'Let's have a look.'

Johnny allowed him to open his jacket and investigate while he himself continued looking at the dead man.

'Hardly broke the skin,' the trooper concluded. 'It'll be sore for a spell but that's about all.' He looked around and addressed the gathering crowd. 'You got a head man in this town? Mayor or something?'

A neat-suited oldster stepped forward. 'That's me, kid. I'm mayor of Logan.'

'State Trooper on official business,' Orlando said, thumbing his badge. 'With your marshal out of action, I'm gonna have to liaise with you. For a start I need use of your law office.'

The dignitary looked grudgingly at the young man then said, 'This way, kid.'

* * *

A group of town officials crowded the small office while at the back Johnny was in a cell. He sat on a bunk, his shirt masking a dressing on his chest.

Veener had just arrived and was standing before the bars looking at him. 'I suddenly realized why you wanted the gun,' she said. 'I was on my way to town when I heard the shooting.'

'You should have stayed out of this, Veener.'

'What's going to happen to you?' she said forlornly.

231

Johnny shook his head resignedly. 'Don't ask.'

Out front Orlando was seated at the marshal's desk and had just glanced through the depositions by witnesses of the day's events. 'Adequate accounts,' he said to the mayor, folding them and putting them into his jacket pocket. 'Thanks for organizing them, Mr Mayor. They'll be needed as evidence. Your co-operation with state police will be put on record.'

'What happens next?'

'I've wired Austin. Following my written report on all this, they'll be sending investigating officers — federals or state police — to make their own enquiries. And, of course, you'll be getting a new marshal. A straight one this time.'

There was a knock at the door and a fellow entered.

The mayor glanced at him. 'Oh, this is the ostler from the livery. Horses ready?'

'Yes, sir.'

'They provisioned?' the trooper asked.

'Yes, sir.'

'Thanks, mister.'

The man touched his forehead and left.

Orlando rose. 'And thank you, gentlemen. Now, if you'll excuse me, I got a job to do.' He waited until the room was cleared then walked to the cell. He opened the door and instructed his prisoner to put out his wrists.

Johnny did so, feeling the cold steel once more clamping shut. 'Austin?'

'Austin. And I'm used to your tricks now, so this time we're gonna make it.'

'Then a rope?' Johnny said, a degree of hopelessness for the first time evident in his voice.

Orlando shrugged. 'I doubt it.'

Johnny was surprised. 'How come?'

Orlando led him to the front, with Veener following quietly. 'I never did think that you shot that bank man.'

'Hell, I told you I didn't. But nobody believed me. The killing had the look of Wallace stamped all over it but I got no case now he's gone. You know, an evil bastard can die but the effects of his doings can live on.'

'Hey, don't give up hope so easy. Can't you see? The state ain't got much case either. What they got against you is only circumstantial and full of loopholes. Nobody actually saw you kill the bank man. You weren't wearing a holster. I've already asked some questions here in Logan and there are witnesses to say it wasn't your habit to tote a gun. Then we've got all that happened here today that testifies to what kind of hardcases the Wallace gang were. I'm sure a jury would think twice before voting you guilty on that kind of evidence. Too many loopholes.'

'Fact is I was found with the corpse and a warm gun near my hand. Seems to me that's what'll count.'

'Not if someone speaks for you.'

'Speaks for me? Such as who?'

'Such as me.'

'But you're a lawman. You ain't got cause to speak up for a criminal.' His voice lowered. ''Sides, you and me ain't the best of friends, Trooper. I've given you one heap of trouble.'

Orlando grinned and his teeth flashed. 'I know you have, you son of a gun. But when we get to Austin I'm gonna give evidence on your behalf. The word of a state trooper will count for something in court.'

He caught the look in his prisoner's eye and chuckled. 'Yeah, even if he is a damn Yankee.'

Johnny couldn't believe what he was hearing. 'You'd do that — for me?'

Orlando shrugged. 'Ain't gonna kid you it'll be plain sailing. And, naturally, you'll do time for robbery. Ain't no way of avoiding that, Reb. But, if they listen to me, and I'm sure they will, there'll be no rope. We'll pull in a good lawyer. Make sure he's not just a shyster going through the motions.'

A look of relief swept over Veener's face. 'I'll wait for you, Johnny.'

Johnny put his cuffed arms over the small figure and held her close for a second. 'We'll see, Veener. Don't be rash. There's a lotta water to go under the bridge yet.'

He disentangled his arms and looked at the Yankee face. His eyes fell to the badge on the man's chest, then returned to the face. This man was the only hope he had. Things went through his mind; the way he had despised Yanks as the enemy; how he had detested them more with the way they had been lording it over their defeated foe, his beloved Texas. Up till this moment he wouldn't have given any one of them the time of day.

He nodded in acceptance of some kind of change that was beginning inside him and allowed himself to be led outside to the waiting horses.

RIDERS OF RIFLE RANGE
Wade Hamilton

Veterinarian Jeff Jones did not like open warfare — but it was there on Scrub Pine grass. When he diagnosed a sick bull on the Endicott ranch as having the contagious blackleg disease, he got involved in the warfare — whether he liked it or not!

BEAR PAW
Nevada Carter

Austin Dailey traded two cows to a pair of Indians for a bay horse, which subsequently disappeared. Tracks led to a secret hideout of fugitive Indians — and cattle thieves. Indians and stockmen co-operated against the rustlers. But it was Pale Woman who acted as interpreter between her people and the rangemen.

THE WEST WITCH
Lance Howard

Detective Quinton Hilcrest journeys west, seeking the Black Hood Bandits' lost fortune. Within hours of arriving in Hags Bend, he is fighting for his life, ensnared with a beautiful outcast the town claims is a witch! Can he save the young woman from the angry mob?

GUNS OF THE PONY EXPRESS
T. M. Dolan

Rich Zennor joined the Pony Express venture at the start, as second-in-command to tough Denning Hartman. But Zennor had the problems of Hartman believing that they had crossed trails in the past, and the fact that he was strongly attached to Hartman's Indian girl, Conchita.

BLACK JO OF THE PECOS
Jeff Blaine

Nobody knew where Black Josephine Callard came from or whither she returned. Deputy U.S. Marshal Frank Haggard would have to exercise all his cunning and ability to stay alive before he could defeat her highly successful gang and solve the mystery.

RIDE FOR YOUR LIFE
Johnny Mack Bride

They rode west, hoping for a new start. Then they met another broken-down casualty of war, and he had a plan that might deliver them from despair. But the only men who would attempt it would be the truly brave — or the desperate. They were both.

THE NIGHTHAWK
Charles Burnham

While John Baxter sat looking at the ruin that arsonists had made of his log house, a stranger rode into the yard. Baxter and Walt Showalter partnered up and re-built the house. But when it was dynamited, they struck back — and all hell broke loose.

MAVERICK PREACHER
M. Duggan

Clay Purnell was hopeful that his posting to Capra would be peaceable enough. However, on his very first day in town he rode into trouble. Although loath to use his .45, Clay found he had little choice — and his likeness to a notorious bank robber didn't help either!

SIXGUN SHOWDOWN
Art Flynn

After years as a lawman elsewhere, Dan Herrick returned to his old Arizona stamping ground to find that nesters were being driven from their homesteads by ruthless ranchers. Before putting away his gun once and for all, Dan forced a bloody and decisive showdown.

RIDE LIKE THE DEVIL!
Sam Gort

Ben Trunch arrived back on the Big T only to find that land-grabbing was in progress. He confronted Luke Fletcher, saloon-keeper and town boss, with what was happening, and was immediately forced to ride for his life. But he got the chance to put it all right in the end.

SLOW WOLF AND DAN FOX:
Larry & Stretch
Marshall Grover

The deck was stacked against an innocent man. Larry Valentine played detective, and his investigation propelled the Texas Trouble-Shooters into a gun-blazing fight to the finish.

BRANAGAN'S LAW
Alan Irwin

To Angus Flint, the valley was his domain and he didn't want any new settlers. But Texas Ranger Jim Branagan had other ideas. Could he put an end to Flint's tyranny for good?

THE DEVIL RODE A PINTO
Bret Rey

When a settler is cut to ribbons in a frenzied attack, Texas Ranger Sam Buck learns that the killer is Rufus Berry, known as The Devil. Sam stiffens his resolve to kill or capture Berry and break up his gang.

THE DEATH MAN
Lee F. Gregson

The hardest of men went in fear of Ford, the bounty hunter, who had earned the name 'The Death Man'. Yet even Ford was not infallible — when he killed the wrong man, he found that he was being sought himself by the feared Frank Ambler.

LEAD LANGUAGE
Gene Tuttle

After Blaze Colton and Ricky Rawlings have delivered a train load of cows from Arizona to San Francisco, they become involved in a load of trouble and find themselves on the run!

A DOLLAR FROM THE STAGE
Bill Morrison

Young saddle-tramp Len Finch stumbled into a web of murder, lawlessness, intrigue and evil ambition. In the end, he put his life on the line for the folks that he cared about.

BRAND 2: HARDCASE
Neil Hunter

When Ben Wyatt and his gang hold up the bank in Adobe, Wyatt is captured. Judge Rice asks Jason Brand, an ex-U.S. Marshal, to take up the silver star. Wyatt is in the cells, his men close by, and Brand is the only man to get Adobe out of real trouble . . .

THE GUNMAN AND THE ACTRESS
Chap O'Keefe

To be paid a heap of money just for protecting a fancy French actress and her troupe of players didn't seem that difficult — but Joshua Dillard hadn't banked on the charms of the actress, and the fact that someone didn't want him even to reach the town . . .

HE RODE WITH QUANTRILL
Terry Murphy

Following the break-up of Quantrill's Raiders, both Jesse James and Mel Becher head their own gang. A decade later, their paths cross again when, unknowingly, they plan to rob the same bank — leading to a violent confrontation between Becher and James.

THE CLOVERLEAF CATTLE COMPANY
Lauran Paine

Bessie Thomas believed in miracles, and her husband, Jawn Henry, did not. But after finding a murdered settler and his woman, and running down the rencgades responsible, Jawn Henry would have time to reflect. He and Bessie had never had children. Miracles evidently did happen.

COOGAN'S QUEST
J. P. Weston

Coogan came down from Wyoming on the trail of a man he had vowed to kill — Red Sheene, known as The Butcher. It was the kidnap of Marian De Quincey that gave Coogan his chance — but he was to need help from an unexpected quarter to avoid losing his own life.

DEATH COMES TO ROCK SPRINGS
Steven Gray

Jarrod Kilkline is in trouble with the army, the law, and a bounty hunter. Fleeing from capture, he rescues Brian Tyler, who has been left for dead by the three Jackson brothers. But when the Jacksons reappear on the scene, will Jarrod side with them or with the law in the final showdown?

GHOST TOWN
J. D. Kincaid

A snowstorm drove a motley collection of individuals to seek shelter in the ghost town of Silver Seam. When violence erupted, Kentuckian gunfighter Jack Stone needed all his deadly skills to secure his and an Indian girl's survival.

INCIDENT AT
LAUGHING WATER CREEK
Harry Jay Thorn

All Kate Decker wants is to run her cattle along Laughing Water Creek. But Leland MacShane and Dave Winters want the whole valley to themselves, and they've hired an army of gunhawks to back their play. Then Frank Corcoran rides right into the middle of it . . .